Over What Hill?

G·K
Hall
&Co

*Also by Effie Leland Wilder
in Large Print:*

Out to Pasture

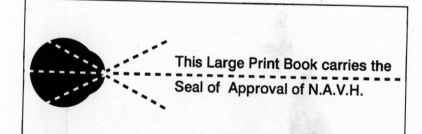

This Large Print Book carries the
Seal of Approval of N.A.V.H.

To
Allison, Frances,
John, and Leland
(Progeny of whom it is easy to be proud)

A Heartfelt Thank You

If I were not so old I might have kept a careful list of all the dear people who furnished me with funny stories for this volume. Rather than leave anyone out, I thank them herewith in a body. I hope they know that I will be eternally grateful.

I'm indebted also to the amazing number of people who wrote words of praise, and who encouraged me to "do another."

I'm grateful to Marian Lord, who bravely served again as my "book editor," for her prodding, her bright ideas, and her calmness and patience in dealing with an antediluvian.

Special thanks go to James J. Kilpatrick, the country's most erudite and beloved word-and-phrase man. To my delight, he "took a shine" to my little novel, *Out to Pasture*, and he let the world know it. His nationwide coverage resulted in many sales, which caused the publisher to want a sequel. Blessings on J. J. K.

E. L. W.

Important

Dear Reader:

Even though this story is called a novel, please don't look for a substantial plot, or for it to thicken.

You see, an involved plot would take too much energy for me to work out, at my age. Also, not many dramatic or consequential things happen here at The Home. It's exciting enough when Dr. Raney comes over to cut our toenails, or when the Country Store gets in a new flavor of ice cream, or when The Home takes us in the bus to the polling place. (Sometimes we have no idea who we're voting for, but it's kind of fun to press the button and know that Our Vote Counts.)

So please don't keep waiting for complications and unravelings thereof. If you can't develop and sustain an interest in the prosaic affairs of a bunch of old codgers who're just trying to get along, on the last leg of their journey, don't read any further. However, my hope is that you will stay with us and get a few laughs, and maybe feel touched a time or two.

Yours,
E. L. W.

Contents

Chapter 1

Dog Days

August 4th

People seem to sniff romance in the air, here at The Home. Even though Retta is doing nothing to promote anything, interest is rife in such questions as: Will Sidney get her? Is she playing too hard to get? How long can he keep up the courting at our time of life?

Sidney is seventy-five, after all, and so is Henrietta.

Henrietta — or Retta, as I've always called her — and I were college classmates back in the dark ages. We had "kept up," and I was delighted when she finally decided to come to FairAcres Retirement Home. I like to think that it was partly because I was here that she made up her mind to apply for an apartment. The only thing is, I now feel that it behooves me to make sure that she likes the place.

Most of the female residents made a special

effort to welcome my old friend, and they seemed to enjoy her — that is, *until* her loveliness began to register on Sidney Metcalf, the unelected, but undisputed, Most Eligible Widower of FairAcres.

Henrietta Gooding has "kept her neck," as the saying goes. Few women in their seventies can make that claim. (Retta doesn't make the claim herself, but it's plain to see.) Where the rest of us have sags and wattles and dewlaps, she has firm contours. A photographer can approach her from any angle without being told, "Please, no side views."

Retta's pleasing profile goes along with the rest of her: a slender, pretty, slightly blue-haired lady whose composure makes it restful to be around her.

The ladies here had long since given up on anybody catching Sidney. Oh, certain sprightly widows had made a mighty effort. I overheard such unsubtle overtures as, "Sidney, do you play RummiKub? We could use a fourth this afternoon."

Or, "Sidney, I happen to have two tickets for the symphony in Charleston on Saturday."

Or, "Sidney, I'm trying to decide if I should sell some of my stocks and buy others. You know so much about the stock market, I was hoping . . ."

It's a wonder he didn't get fat from all the brownies and lemon squares and other goodies that were made in tiny kitchens and presented to him on dainty napkins.

Sidney fended them off politely, like the Southern gentleman he is. The ladies finally decided that his devotion to his dead wife's memory made him invulnerable.

That was before Retta.

She crooked no finger; she winked no eye; she baked no tart. She made no effort to sit near him in any gathering. Maybe that's why *he* began to make an effort. He would manage to get to our little post office at the same time she did, and help get her mail out of a box that was too high up for her. He would wait in front of the chapel every Sunday morning until she arrived, and then he would walk in to the service with her proudly.

He even asked her to play golf with him at the Drayton Country Club. Retta declared that she had never played, and didn't even know a niblick from a niblet. He assured her that it would be his pleasure to teach her.

Retta came to me, troubled. "Hattie, you know I'm not athletic. I only made one D at Converse College, and that was in Phys. Ed. I couldn't crawl through the horizontal ladders, much less make any of the teams. Playing tiddledywinks is about my speed. . . . I don't want people to see me swing and swing and dig a hole in the turf, trying to make that little old ball pop up."

"Why don't you tell him you'll ride in his golf cart and help him spot balls, but won't swing at one?" I suggested.

That's what she did, and apparently they had

15

a fine afternoon. Retta says she knows she looked out of place on the golf course in her large, straw garden-party hat. "I can't help it," she said. "Rather ridicule than sunburn."

Her below-the-knee skirt may have raised some eyebrows, too. Isn't it something? When we were young, a woman out in public in shorts was an immodest oddity. Now it's a skirt that looks strange on the greens! *O tempera, O mores.* (I'm sure it's not hard to guess which "time" and which "manners" *I* prefer.)

Sidney asked Retta to make the golf excursion a regular thing, three times a week. She said no. "Once a month — and only when the weather is fine and I'm feeling fair to middlin'."

Sidney even finagled around and had his place in the dining room changed to her table. And that's how things stand as of this writing.

A few of the men are making book on the affair, some betting that bells will ring before Christmas, others that Sidney will come to his senses before Thanksgiving. I suppose this interest in Cupid's activities is better than just sitting around watching the brown spots get bigger on the backs of our hands.

August 7th

Golf seems to be of particular interest around here. All summer, several of the male residents have been requesting that The Home make a putting green. It was finally decided that this could

16

Sidney asked Retta to make the golf excursion a regular thing, three times a week.

17

be done in the East Courtyard. A few plants would have to be moved, but not enough to make a grave difference in the landscaping, the administration decided. However, the powers that be reckoned without the ladies on G Hall, which adjoins and looks out on that courtyard.

"They will break all our windows!" one lady wailed. She was not completely mollified by the explanation that the men would not be driving the balls — just pushing them gently toward little holes.

Another lady exclaimed, "It's an invasion of our privacy! We'll have men peering at us through our windows all day long, no matter how we're dressed — or undressed!"

"Don't you wish!" one sassy man muttered, *sotto voce.*

Anyway, the Putting Green Project is going ahead. Mr. Detwiler, our head man, has decided to please the golfing enthusiasts this time, and to close his ears to the complaints. I admire him for it.

August 9th

Not for any amount of money would I be the administrator of an old folks' home. The wear and tear on my already imperfect disposition would be fatal.

Our Mr. Detwiler manages to survive, even to smile sometimes; but there are signs of combat fatigue. One of his eyes twitches at times, and I have seen him knot the fingers of his right hand together, and then close his left hand over the fist, as if to keep it from committing some sort of violence.

I was in Mr. Detwiler's office today, reporting on the Residents' Council meeting. When I got to the part about Geneva Tinken stating stridently that somebody was filching her guava juice from where she had hidden it in a bottle inside a bag in the back of the top shelf of the C-Hall refrigerator ("I put a mark on the bottle, and it's two inches down!"), he hit the ceiling.

"Miss Hattie," he said — he's years younger than I am, and Southern in his politeness — "that's the kind of picayune complaint that's about to do me in. That's the kind of petty griping I have to listen to, day in and day out. Do you know what I've decided? I think there ought to be a test for everyone to take before they can get into this place, a test that would give us some idea of how contrary they are —"

"I know what you mean!" I broke in. "Instead of an I.Q. test, it would be a C.Q. test: Contrariness Quotient!"

"Right!" Mr. Detwiler said. "You've hit the nail on the head. I'll tell you what let's do, Miss Hattie. Let's give the matter some serious thought and start making out questions. Will you help me do that? Make out some questions for a C.Q. test?"

I said I'd be glad to.

As I got up to leave his office, Mr. D. said,

"Have you heard anything from that publishing house in Atlanta?"

"Not a word."

"How long have they had your manuscript?"

"Twelve weeks." I had told a few people, including our beloved administrator, that I had bundled up the journal I'd been keeping about life at a Southern retirement home and sent it to a publisher. Now I was beginning to be sorry I'd told anybody. "They sent me a card acknowledging receipt, but nothing else. I wish they'd go on and send it back. I enclosed return postage."

"Well, give 'em time. I suppose when you don't have an agent, and they've never heard of you, it takes a little longer."

"I suppose so. I'll let you know first thing, if I get any good news."

"You do that."

August 12th

One of our "inmates" is incensed. She was looking at a bulletin board in the lobby, where book jackets are displayed from the newest books in our library. She saw the cover of a book by Lewis Grizzard — *Don't Bend Over in the Garden, Granny, You Know Them Taters Got Eyes!*

"Disgusting," declared the prim and proper lady, "bawdy, and entirely too titillating!"

Wouldn't Lewis have loved it? He'd have made something out of that "titillating," I'll bet.

August 14th

I couldn't sleep tonight. My mind has skittered and wandered and lit on a face, a face I saw on the eleven o'clock news — that unforgettable face, topped with its odd headdress. A rhyme began to form and now, at two in the morning, I am up and setting down the lines before they flitter away.

FORMS OF PUNISHMENT
You can beat me, you can whip me,
You can tie me to a tree,
You can throw me in the briar patch
And never set me free;

You can make me do a somersault
Or even "skin the cat,"
But *please* don't say I have to kiss
Yasser Arafat!

August 15th

I noticed work in progress on the putting green today. Thinking about the hue and cry that was raised about that matter, it came to me that perhaps a question on the Contrariness Quotient test could be: Are you willing to support — or at least not to oppose — a project that will benefit several people, but not yourself? Even if the project might slightly inconvenience you?

21

August 16th

Today there was a letter in my post office box with an interesting return address in the left-hand corner. My hand shook as I tore open the envelope. This is what was inside:

Mrs. Harriet McNair
FairAcres Home
Drayton, South Carolina

Dear Mrs. McNair:
I have read the manuscript you sent us and enjoyed it very much. We would like to have some biographical material about you. Have you done any other writing? Have you had anything published? Please furnish us with some data on yourself, after which I will approach our marketing department to see if it would be feasible for us to publish your story. I am looking forward to hearing from you.
                              Yours very truly,
                              David Lowman
                              Managing Editor

Whoo-eeee! I could hardly fold the letter and get it back into the envelope. I was shaking a little. Should I tell anybody? No. He said they're just *thinking* about publishing. There is no commitment. I'd better not get a hullabaloo started. I'd better just do what the man asked, quietly.

They know nothing about me, except that since I live in a retirement home (my return address told them that) I must be old. They might think they're dealing with some kind of a witch.

Somebody needs to write them besides me. Whose opinion would they respect?

I thought at once about Bob Crawford, editor of Drayton's twice-a-week paper. I had written a few feature articles for Bob, and we had become friendly. I called him and begged him please to write those publishers and tell them I am not a witch. He laughed and readily agreed to do so.

Then I got to thinking: What do they really want from me? A résumé? A photograph? I decided to stick my neck out and call Mr. Lowman. When I finally got through to him I felt intimidated, and he didn't help me. After a minute or two I said, "You're not from the South, are you?"

"No, ma'am," he said — No, now that I think about it, he didn't say "ma'am." He said, "No, I'm from Boston — but I like your stuff!"

And I began to like that Yankee man.

From what he told me I realized that he was pulling for me against several in the organization who thought that printing my novel was too great a risk. Printing costs being what they are, as Mr. Lowman explained, their company couldn't often afford to take a chance on one of the thousands of unsolicited manuscripts people send them every year.

I can understand their fear. I am an utterly

unknown writer with no following, no reputation. Why should they take a chance on an unpublished lady whose only claim to fame is that she has survived for an astonishing number of decades?

I was so eager to hear from them, and now that I have, I'm a bundle of nerves. It reminds me of something I overheard at lunch today: "I wish I could get it all together . . . but, I don't know . . . If I did get it all together, I wouldn't know what to do with it!" My sentiments exactly!

August 20th

A young man, visiting, sang a haunting solo in church this morning: "It Is Well, It Is Well With My Soul." His conviction was evident. I wish I could feel as sure about my soul as he does about his.

August 21st

You would have had to be there. I'm afraid it won't sound funny in the telling, but I'll try. It seems to take such small things to send us into gales of laughter.

Monday nights they show old movies in the dining room. Tonight it was a Nelson Eddy–Jeanette MacDonald extravaganza set in the Canadian Rockies. Several residents in the audience nodded off almost before the opening credits finished, including Mary Endicott, who had been rolled in from the infirmary in her wheelchair.

The scenery was magnificent and the music wonderful, but I began to think that the colors were just too brilliant, that Jeanette's coiffure was too perfect, that Nelson's uniform was too shiny-clean. Funny, it hadn't seemed so fifty years ago!

A while later, Nelson Eddy knocked on a log-cabin door. There was no answer. He raised his arms and banged again with all his might: bam-Bam-BAM! Mary Endicott jerked up, raised her head, and yelled, "Come in!"

It was the best moment of the evening.

August 23rd

Mr. Lowman wrote to thank me for the information I sent and asked in his letter if the manuscript was "on disk," or if I could put it "on disk," using IBM or Macintosh. I wrote him back this afternoon that I had no idea what he was talking about. I'm sure he will sigh when he reads that.

Will this be the end of my little book? Will they publish it, or not? The decision remains in limbo, and I am having a time trying to possess my soul in patience — trying not to tell anybody that my novel is even being considered. It is against my nature to keep such a secret. If something isn't decided soon, I'm liable to explode.

I can't seem to get poor Mr. Detwiler and his troubles off my mind.

One of the hardest things he has to do is arbitrate disputes between the residents. Susan Willoughby evidently kicked up quite a fuss last Friday. Susan (not the pleasantest soul in this habitation) lives alone in one of The Home's cottages. In the next cottage lives Cecil Canaday, and in front of his cottage sits his large camper, a little more on her side of the grass than on his, which is a bone of contention.

Susan caught Cecil plugging an electric cord from his camper into an outlet on the front of her house. She yelled bloody murder.

"Well, ma'am, don't blow my head off," said Cecil in his nice Lowcountry voice. "Your outlet just happens to be a little closer to my camper than mine. Anyway, The Home pays the electric bill."

"I don't care who pays it," Susan insisted. "That receptacle is for my use exclusively. I shall report this incident to Mr. Detwiler."

Which she did — at 4:45 on Friday afternoon, when Mr. D. was probably trying to get loose to do a little fishing. I'm sure his left eyelid was doing a job of twitching before he got Susan calmed down by promising to give Cecil a good scolding.

I can just hear Mr. D. saying to himself: "I don't *want* to give Cecil a scolding. I *like* Cecil.

His Contrariness Quotient is high in my book —
on the good side. Her C.Q. is a D minus — on
the bad side."

Reading back a few pages in this journal, it
seems that I am being hard on the women residents. There are a few cantankerous females here,
but there are many more quiet, gentle, helpful
ones.

Rose Hibben, for instance. She suffers from
asthma, but she is always finding ways to help
people who are worse off than herself.

This afternoon I ran into her in the gazebo at
the duck pond, where she had pushed Emma
Moore. Emma has been confined to bed-and-
wheelchair for several years. Her husband died
last year, and her children are far away. So,
unless some kind soul volunteers, there is usually
no one to take her out on a pretty day — to
give her some relief from the monotony of the
Health Care Center. (That's what we are now
asked to call it. I'm afraid it will always be "the
infirmary" in my mind.)

Today had that hint of autumn that is so re-
freshing at the end of our summers. We sat quietly, listening to a mockingbird who apparently
liked this day as much as we did, and was letting
the world know it.

After a while Rose said, "I just thought of a
funny story. Miss Emma, will you let me tell a

story with a bad word in it?"

Miss Emma smiled. "Two bad words, if you need them."

"OK. We had a minister at home who swore this happened to him. He asked the children in the congregation to come to the front for a children's sermon. Suzy led the pack, dancing down the aisle, proudly smoothing down the ruffles of her starched white organdy dress. The minister felt compelled to comment.

" 'My, that's a pretty dress, Suzy.'

" 'Thank you. I think so too.' Then, in a voice loud enough for all to hear, she added, 'But Mama says it's a *bitch* to iron!' "

We doubled up, laughing. We drowned out the bird with our whoops.

August 28th

Ellen Caine kept us so amused at the table today that we could hardly eat. She told us about the time in the fourth grade when the teacher sent her on an errand. She did the errand and then loitered in the hall, enjoying her freedom from the classroom.

A tall, strict, elderly teacher appeared and glared at Ellen. Miss Adams muttered something about idle children, and Ellen started running down the hall. The teacher called out, "The wicked flee where no man pursueth!"

At recess, Ellen said, she told her best friend about the encounter. "Miss Adams scared me."

"What did she say?"

"Something about a 'wicked flea.' "

August 29th

Several people at The Home go in pairs once a week to deliver meals for the local Meals on Wheels program. Sidney Metcalf, in particular, has seemed to enjoy the task, and to enjoy the companionship of his partner, Austin Craver.

Austin recently slipped on a muddy path out near the duck pond and broke his ankle. It is such a bad break that he knows he will be out of commission for a long time; so he told Sid he'd better get another partner. Sidney immediately approached Retta.

"Meals on Wheels? I don't know anything about it," she responded. "They didn't have it in my hometown."

"Well, that's too bad, because it's a great service. We take hot, nourishing midday meals to people who are housebound — from age or sickness or infirmity — and have no one to help them. The folks I deliver to are real nice people, and I have found it to be very rewarding. Won't you take Austin's place? Won't you be my MOW partner?"

"Once a week? I don't know . . . I hate to tie myself down."

Sidney looked so crestfallen that Retta relented. "I'll tell you what. I'll go with you one time and try it out."

So Sidney has added charitable works to his courtship strategy. I'm not sure you can get stars in your crown that way! Perhaps we should check and see if Sidney was anywhere near Austin when he fell at the duck pond!

August 30th

Gusta Barton is always colorful in her speech, but not always very tasteful or ladylike. Yesterday she was telling some of us about a man in her hometown — a "paragon," she claims. (There seem to be a lot of those where she comes from.)

She said, "Everything he tries works out. Everything he plants grows — and if he steps in something, it smells good on him!"

September 1st

Today, at last, came a wonderful phone call. It was Mr. Lowman, calling from Atlanta.

"You're in!" he said, sounding almost like a Southerner. "We're going to publish your book!"

He went on to tell me that it was something of a miracle because their company receives an average of eighteen thousand manuscripts a year, out of which they publish fifteen to twenty books. Most of the published ones come from agents or authors they know. I had no agent, no introduction.

"You have a darn good story though, Mrs. McNair, and it's in an area that hasn't been

plumbed. I can't remember reading another book about a retirement home."

He told me that publication would probably take place in December. That seemed a long way off.

Chapter 2

Ties That Bind

September 11th

I floated around on Cloud Nine for days. Visions of sugar plums — royalties, that is — danced in my head. There was the business of signing my first contract. What a thrill!

Then today came a blow. Mr. Lowman called. I could tell something was wrong. *They can't back out now. I've got a contract.*

"I hate to tell you," he said, "but we have to postpone publication until the spring."

Oh, no! I have told everybody in the world when the launching would be — Already impossibly far away, and now months longer! I told Mr. Lowman that he couldn't do me that way. But, of course, he could.

"We're a small organization," he said, "and we give each book personal attention. We simply haven't the personnel to do a rush job. We want to produce your book properly. You'll be glad —

when it comes out."

Like fun. "I just hope I'm still here when it comes out," I said, forlornly. He declared that he hoped so, too, and we hung up on that sad note.

September 12th

Six of us — four players and two kibitzers — were enjoying RummiKub in the C-Hall parlor this afternoon, and we got to talking about divorce. We agreed that it had reached worrisome proportions. So different from the time of our youth, when a divorced person was an oddity, and just a little bit "beyond the pale."

"I went home last year to a big wedding in my church," said Tilly Horton. "Had a grand time. Saw everybody I ever knew. It was a beautiful wedding. The bridesmaids were pretty, and they didn't wear black or navy blue, which seems to be in style now. They wore what we used to call 'ashes of roses,' a soft, becoming shade.

"The bride and groom looked like they could eat each other up. They swore up and down and sideways to love and honor and cherish. But do you know something? Those kids broke up before they finished thanking people for the presents! I never did get a note about my cup and saucer. It was the good pattern, too — not the everyday one."

We shook our heads over Tilly's story. All of us could have told similar ones. Several in the group have children whose marriages have gone on the rocks.

"It's a plague," said Cora Hunter. "It worries me a lot. . . . Of course, I know there are cases where divorce is necessary — absolutely the only solution. But I'm talking about the epidemic of breakups: three marriages out of five. I think that's the count. Isn't that awful? . . . I've often thought that there should be a course that couples have to take, and a test they have to pass, before they marry. Something that would clue them in to the hardships . . . the rough spots . . . the disappointments —"

"I know what you mean, Cora," said Christine. "Oooh, those disappointments! Honey, I almost ran home to Mama about seventeen times the first six months. Every time Phil looked at me even a little bit cockeyed, I'd start to bawl. I was a spoiled-rotten mess. I thought it was all gonna be moonlight and roses."

"But you stuck it out?" someone asked.

"Sure I did. I wasn't gonna go crawlin' home, to be pitied. Besides, I might not've been welcome. My parents would most probably have said, 'Look here, Missy. You made solemn promises, before God and that company!' So I stuck it out, and things got better. We gradually learned how to give and take. I guess it turned out we had a little bit of character after all. We learned how to laugh at a lot of things we used to get huffy about. But today, couples don't stick it out. It seems to me they don't try to rationalize

anything. Two or three little tiffs, and, bingo! Split City!"

Somebody said, "I wonder how the lawyers who do all the splitting feel. I wonder if they ever think about those words, 'let no man put asunder.' "

We played for a while, quietly. At the next break, Christine said, "I think you've got something, Cora. If I had taken a course in 'How It's *Really* Going to Be, after the Honeymoon,' I believe I might have been spared a lot of tears and heartache."

Cora said, "They could call it, 'When Moonlight and Roses Turn into Dark Clouds and Dishwater.' "

Just then the supper bell rang, putting an end to our disquieting discourse.

September 13th

There was a windstorm last night — maybe a small tornado — that tore into some buildings not far from The Home. We felt it enough to get a little frightened, but we weren't in the direct path, thank goodness.

Talking about the storm today reminded Ethel Fisher of something that happened when she was a child, living on a farm. A tornado hit her family's windmill, sending it crashing into the commissary, where the year's "crop" of cane syrup was stored. All the jugs broke open, and in a few minutes the whole backyard was inches deep in the sticky mess. Ethel said you couldn't step off the back porch without being up to your ankles in gooey syrup.

She laughed. "It even got into the chicken yard. You should've seen the hens and rooster stepping high and kicking their legs, trying to shake off the stuff."

She couldn't remember how they got rid of it. Said she thought they just had to wait for the Lord to send a hard rain. She also said she'd never liked cane syrup much after that. It always made her feet start to feel kind of sticky!

I love to hear tales like that, about days that are gone and will never return.

September 14th

I ran into Arthur Priest, the bulwark of our maintenance department, in the hall, and asked if his house had been damaged by the storm.

"The yard's a mess, from fallen limbs — but that's easy to clear up," he reported. "The house didn't even shiver. That's a strong bugger — excuse me, ma'am — a strong house, Miz McNair. Dollie and I are surely grateful for the place and to all of you who found it for us."

"I'll bet the house is glad you all are in it!" I said, and walked on.

It was just about a year ago that some of us were concerned about a place for Arthur's burgeoning family to live. Like the answer to a prayer, four of us, out for an afternoon walk,

36

investigated a wooded area about half a mile from The Home and found a house that was not only abandoned, but was choking under a vicious onslaught of kudzu vine. We named it Kudzu Kottage, found its cantankerous owner, and with much difficulty persuaded him to rent it to Arthur and Dollie, who are now in the process of buying it.

I straightened my shoulders and walked a little more proudly. Thinking about getting that nice little family settled, so happily, did me good. Maybe busybody genes aren't so bad, after all.

September 15th

Retta came to my apartment this afternoon to report on her first Meals-on-Wheels delivery yesterday.

"It was interesting!" she declared. "We had to report to the Episcopal Church's kitchen and line up to be given our lunches, which Sidney put in his big cooler — or warmer, in this case. In the car, I peeped into one of the containers and found beef stew, potatoes, green beans, and a roll. It smelled good."

"I know," I said. "It did on the occasions that I helped them out, too."

"The first person we delivered to was Mamie Somebody, a dear little black woman, crippled now, who had been an elementary school teacher. She never married and is utterly alone. She kept thanking and thanking us. She was standing in the front doorway on her crutches, waiting for us — glad to see somebody."

"I think the social contact is almost as important as the food," I remarked.

"She also kept thanking Sidney for fixing her front steps. It seems he went back on two afternoons last week and mended her broken steps, so she wouldn't have an accident."

"Um *hummmm*," I said. "It seems he finds time to do a few things besides courting."

"Oh, Hattie, *do*. . . . Anyway, we took meals to three other people where we visited briefly — nothing out of the ordinary. Then the last stop was interesting."

"How so?"

"Well, the man lives alone, and he's a veteran of World War II. He has congestive heart trouble, but he doesn't want to be in a veterans' hospital or a home. Sidney says it's probably because they wouldn't let him smoke.

"Anyway, his name is Ben Stringfellow, and he has a wonderful sense of humor. He and Sidney are great pals. And, oh, Hattie, while we were talking to Ben on his porch I spied four big eyes looking at us through the fence of the next yard: Jeffrey — he's about five — and Jamie, about three. Little waifs. Ben says there's no father in the picture. Their mother works, and their grandmother is supposed to be tending them, but, Ben says, she mostly tends her gin bottle. So they are at the fence or in Ben's house most of the time. I never saw two sweeter looking little brothers. I

38

can't get them off my mind."

"Does that mean you'll deliver with Sidney again next week?" I inquired.

"I guess it does. I'd like to take those children something. . . . I looked in their yard, and there was not one thing for them to play with."

September 16th

I've been missing "overheard" stories told by Paul and Curtis. They haven't been having their after-supper sessions on the terrace lately, because Paul has been sick. But tonight they were back at their old haunt, and I was sitting at my old place near the library window, through which I could hear them.

"I sure miss baseball. This strike makes me right angry," Paul said.

"Me, too," agreed Curtis. "I really miss the Braves."

"Man! I was sure they would win the Series this year!"

"I heard a pretty good baseball story at the drugstore today," Curtis said. "Want to hear it?"

"Sure."

"Well, it's about two guys named Joe and Larry who had played baseball when they were young, and who liked the game as much as you and I do. When Larry became deathly ill, all he could talk about was whether or not there would be baseball in heaven. 'I'll tell you what, Joe,' he whispered, 'I'll find some way to communicate

"... I never saw two sweeter looking little brothers. I can't get them off my mind."

40

with you and let you know about the game up there.' Joe nodded, brushing away the tears.

"Then weeks after Larry's death, when there had been no communication, Joe decided to do something about the matter. He went to see a medium and arranged a séance. After some difficulty, the medium managed to put the two men in touch. Larry's voice sounded happy.

" 'It's pretty nice up here, Joe. And I've got some good news for you, and something you may consider bad news.'

" 'Let me have it, Larry,' said Joe.

" 'Well, the good news is: we have wonderful baseball up here. I'm enjoyin' playin' again. . . . The bad news is: you're scheduled to pitch tonight!' "

Paul, Curtis, and I all had a good laugh.

September 28th

Retta has been on the route with Sidney for three Wednesdays now. Each time she has come home full of talk about "the waifs" — how adorable they are, how good Jeffrey is to his little brother. She gets a special look in her eyes when she talks about the older boy. Retta's only child, a gentle little son, died of meningitis when he was six.

Today she said, "I can't help being impressed by how kind Sidney is to all the people he takes meals to. They seem to love him."

"Hm-m-m," I said. That, and nothing more, I swear.

41

September 29th

Today I was in the library, catching up on some of the magazines The Home subscribes to, and I heard Paul and Curtis just outside on the terrace swapping stories again.

Curtis told about visiting his children and watching an old movie on television one afternoon with his seven-year-old grandson, Travis.

"The leading lady and her beau had arrived back at her place in full evening dress, and she said, 'I think I'll go and change into something else.'

"Travis poked me in the side and said, 'I bet she changes into a dog!' "

The two pals didn't know that I had a good laugh along with them on the other side of the window.

"When the heroine returned," Curtis continued, "she had on a black satin negligee — really racy for those days."

"I know what you mean," Paul laughed. "My children are embarrassed to go to any of today's movies with me because of the language and the lovemaking — though I'm not sure that's the right word for it!"

I certainly know what they mean about today's questionable "entertainment."

September 30th

Every now and then The Home takes residents

— any who want to go shopping — to a large mall about fifteen miles away. Our two bus drivers, June and Ophelia, are models of patience on these trips. They tell us to set our watches, and to come back to the bus in exactly two hours.

On a recent trip Geneva turned to her seatmate, Emily Jenkins, and said, "Don't worry, dear. It's a big mall, and it's easy to get lost in, but I'll take care of you."

Emily, a quiet soul, said nothing. She neither wanted nor needed the bossy Geneva's supervision. All she wanted was three pairs of Soft Taupe Thigh-High stockings from Sears, size Shapely.

When the two hours were up, everyone was back on the bus except Geneva. Emily had managed to elude her in Sears by slipping into the restroom, and then sneaking down aisles between high piles of bedspreads and draperies, and then out to the bus.

Geneva, meanwhile, was frantic. She had offered to protect someone she considered inferior in judgment, and she had failed. She did not like to fail.

She asked one clerk after the other: "Have you seen a little mousy lady with white hair and glasses? In a magenta knit?" They all shook their heads.

While we waited, June and Ophelia searched through Belk's, Woolworth's, and Dillard's before finally capturing Geneva in Sears.

43

When the trio got back to the parking lot, Geneva poked her head into the bus from the top step, stopped, and glared at the passengers.

"Don't you all dare look funny at *me*," she said irately. "*I'm* not lost." She pointed to Emily. "*She's* the one who was lost." And she took her seat in high dudgeon.

How about a C.Q. question something like, "Can you take part in group events without trying to be the boss of everyone else?"

October 10th

Ella Douglas got hold, somehow, of a set of cowbells — an old, authentic set, brassy and loud. She decided they would be the very things to warn her of intruders; so she hung the bells on the inside knob of the door to her apartment.

One night late — in fact, in the middle of the night — Ella heard the bells hit the floor with a loud jangling. She jumped up out of bed, grabbed her walk-around phone, ran into her bathroom, and locked the door. She dialed what she thought was The Home's emergency number, but in her shaken state, she must have pressed a wrong digit.

A woman answered sleepily, "Hello?"

"My cowbells have fallen, and I'm locked in the bathroom!" Ella exclaimed. "Please come!"

"Who *is* this?" the woman asked.

"Ella Douglas. Apartment 209. Help! My cowbells have fallen off the door, and I'm locked in the bathroom —"

The woman slammed down the phone at that point. She probably thought her line had gotten tangled up with one from the state asylum.

It happened.

In the line waiting for lunch today, I heard a lady lose patience with one of our big talkers and say to her: "You talk too much!"

After a short pause, the chatterbox replied: "Well, maybe I do. But I'll tell you something. My tongue is the only thing about me that still works good!"

October 20th

I have been to Atlanta to meet my publishers. It was not David Lowman who called to make the suggestion, and I wondered a little about that. Sure enough, when I got there I learned to my disappointment that I would not get to meet my champion. He had left the company to take a teaching job at a local college; but he sent me his good wishes. I shall always be grateful to him.

I was charmed with all the editors and assistants that I met. They treated their far-oldest author with a very special kindness. I saw dozens of photographs on a wall of one of the offices. "Are those pictures of people whose works you have published?" I asked. When they said yes, I said, "Show me Dr. Ferrol Sams." They did, and his was, of course, the brightest face on the wall.

"Please put my picture right next to his," I requested, and they promised to do so.

I had suggested black-and-white illustrations for the book, to lengthen as well as enhance it. They took me up on the suggestion, and had a young artist to meet me, with several preliminary drawings. I asked her how she got the old people to look so authentic. She said, "I went to a retirement home in Atlanta and took some pictures." Good idea.

They introduced me to Evelyn Hogan, who would be my "book editor."

"You and I will go round-and-round these next few weeks," she said, and how true that is already proving to be!

One of the staff members is going to New York to get the book jacket designed! I wish I could go along, but I'd probably be a fifth wheel, not knowing anything about what sells a book from the outside.

Anyway, these are exciting days for this Poor Old Soul! I wonder what my dear Sam — who used to call me that — would think about all this!

October 25th

The Easons — Edmund and Mollie — are a sweet couple who've been at The Home for at least eight years. I believe they were active when they first came, playing bridge and croquet, serving on the council, helping tend the shrubbery,

46

doing everything together. But her mental clock began winding down two years ago.

Edmund takes beautiful care of her. Every afternoon he pushes her in her wheelchair all around the campus. On rainy days they sit on the porch. She seems content as long as she can reach out and touch him.

Today I sat near them on the porch, waiting for the shower to end so that I could go shopping.

Mollie put her tiny hand on her husband's arm. "Honey," she said, looking up at him, "we've been going together a long, long time, haven't we? Don't you think it's about time we started talking about getting married?"

Edmund glanced at me, a little embarrassed. He knew that I knew that they had three great-grandchildren.

"Yes, sweetheart. You're right. I'll get ready to speak to your . . ." He stopped, probably thinking that in the strange condition of her mind, she might just happen to know that her father was gone, and she might get further confused. "I'll speak to the minister," he said, and patted her arm. She gave him a brilliant smile, and he kissed her hand.

I sat there trying not to cry, which was hard, especially after certain words by a sentimental, long-dead Scotsman popped into my sentimental mind:

John Anderson, my jo, John,
  We clamb the hill thegither;

47

And mony a cantie day, John,
  We've had wi ane anither:
Now we maun totter down, John,
  And hand in hand we'll go,
And sleep thegither at the foot,
  John Anderson, my jo.

"Excuse me," I said, and dashed inside,
blinded by the tears that seem to flow so easily
these days.

Chapter 3

Blessed States

October 26th

At lunch today we were discussing the changing-of-tables routine. We are moved to a different table every two months now. Some people think we should change eating partners oftener than that.

Curtis spoke up. "Well, I'll tell you all something," he said. "It doesn't matter when I move, or to what table: I know that the peas and carrots will always follow me."

Later

People say that some of us have "turned funny." I think a good part of our "funniness" is due to poor hearing. For instance, I overheard this exchange in the lobby today:

"Oh, Mary. Hello. I haven't seen you in a long time."

49

"No, I've been out of it. I had trouble with a bad bug."

"You had trouble with a *bed* bug?"

I, for one, will take laughter where I can find it. A good sense of humor goes a long way to help with a good score on the C.Q. test, I believe, and benefits mental health in general. I agree with whoever called laughter, "internal jogging."

October 27th

As Retta has continued to deliver for Meals on Wheels, I have learned more about Ben String-fellow from her accounts. I invited her for coffee this morning and when she mentioned him, I told her that he intrigued me.

"He does me, too, Hattie," she said. "There's something sweet and wholesome about the old fellow. He's always so clean . . . 'Old,' did I say?" she laughed. "Well, he's about my age, I expect. Sidney says he has mentioned getting a pension — probably a good one. He sends a check every month to Meals on Wheels, for more than the meals cost.

"It seems that Ben was born and raised on a farm a few miles from Highlands, North Carolina. After his Army days, he came down to Charleston and got a job as a carpenter at the Naval Shipyard. He and his wife, who died a few years ago, had no children. Sidney asked him yesterday if he'd considered going back to North Carolina, but he said, 'All that're left there are cousins — and not kissin' cousins. No sirree. Not by a *long* shot.'

"He said he liked the warmth of the Lowcountry. 'I used to set a lotta store by that mountain air, but now it plumb glaciates me.' He shivered when he said it. He not only has a bad heart, but chronic bronchitis, too," Retta explained.

" 'Glaciates.' An unusual word," I said.

"Isn't it? He's full of unusual words. Colorful words. And we found out that he's musical, too. When we got there, he was sitting on the porch, playing his ukulele and singing to amuse his two little visitors — those precious children from next door.

"They were so cute sitting at his feet, learning the words to 'Skip to My Lou, My Darlin'.' You can tell they love to hear him sing, even though he has to stop and cough every few minutes. Their two little blond heads were nodding in time with the music, and Jeffrey was pretending he was playing a ukulele, too."

"A ukulele! When have I thought of one of those? Plinkety-plink-plink."

"Oh," exclaimed Retta, "but he gets real music out of it, like Arthur Godfrey used to do. Remember? And Andy Griffith."

We sat quietly for a few minutes, looking out at some of the lovely autumn colors. Then Retta said, "Hattie, do you know about the picnic that's coming up, at Lucille Taylor's?"

"Yes. I'm so glad she's continued having them."

Lucille Taylor is a great person — a wonderful friend and benefactor of FairAcres Home. Her mother, who was a resident here for a number of years, died in the infirmary last year. Lucille has a house on the banks of Lake Moultrie, and twice a year she invites all residents so inclined to come to the lake for a day of fishing and outdoor enjoyment. It's a popular event.

"Sidney was telling me about The Home taking a full bus load of people, every time, and what fun it is." She hesitated. "I was wondering . . . do you suppose we might ask if we could bring Ben and the little boys?"

"I don't see why not," I answered. "Sidney could even take his car, if the bus is too full."

"Hattie, I haven't met Lucille yet. Would you be willing to ask her?"

"Of course. Why not? I'm sure three more won't make any difference to that hospitable gal. In fact, I'll ask if the Priests can come and bring their children. The boys can play together."

It was good to see Retta looking interested and alert. She had been a bit subdued when she first came, and I had been afraid she might be disappointed in the life *chez* FairAcres. I think now that it was just the trauma of the move, the complete change in her way of life. Two little lonesome children and the generous old man who is trying to help them have taken her mind off of herself and the effort of adjusting to retirement living.

October 28th

There was a full house at our beauty parlor today. There's nothing like a nice shampoo and set to perk a body up. Gladys, our beautician, says that after she has combed out several heads of bushy, white hair, she feels like she's been picking cotton!

October 29th (In the "Wee Hours")

It is one of the ironies of life that in our old age, when we finally have ample time and opportunity for sleep, that blessed state eludes us. We seem to spend a lot of time talking about it, however. "I didn't close my eyes until after four." "I know I didn't sleep three hours last night." "I tossed and turned and wrestled with the bedclothes till all hours." These comments are often heard in the dining room or during those visits near the mail boxes.

(Incidentally, what does "all hours" mean? I know about long hours, endless hours, tiresome hours, even wee hours — but "all hours"?)

I have devised a sleep-inducing method that works — sometimes. Not always. Like tonight — or this morning — when I'm writing this at 4:00 A.M.

I envision a lovely green meadow with a stream running through one side of it. In my mind, I watch and listen to the water as it flows serenely along, under the trees and over the smooth

stones. Slowly I intone these adverbs: *Softly* . . .
gently . . . *quietly* . . . *peacefully.* I say those four
words over and over, as the cool water trickles
and gurgles down its pleasant path in the
meadow.

If I'm lucky, the next thing I know, I've
dropped off in the middle of an adverb . . . and
it's morning.

Of course, another of my diversions for nights
when I can't lull my buzzing brain to rest is
putting down doggerel rhymes:

> The temperature is never right.
> It's either too cool or too hot.
> I think I need an overhaul.
> My thermostat is shot!

Later (At the Other End of the Day)

I did get a few hours of sleep after my "wee
hours" jotting, and I had a lovely, long nap this
afternoon. I should be "in the pink" (wonder
where that phrase came from) for tomorrow's
activities.

October 30th

Today was the lakeside picnic at Lucille Taylor's country place. I'm pleasantly tired and
looking forward to a great snooze after so much
outdoor activity. I don't think I'll have any
trouble sleeping tonight! But first I want to put

down the events while they are fresh in my mind. Nothing spectacular happened; it was just the kind of unspectacular day you like to remember.

Several men and women residents could hardly wait to get out on Lucille's dock. I'm surprised at how many people like to fish. It doesn't interest me in the least — but today I had a special reason to "spectate" that sport.

Sidney and Retta each held onto a little boy, each of whom had been outfitted in new tennis shoes, jeans, and plaid shirts. Ben Stringfellow carried the poles and the bait. I sat in a deck chair on the bank, near enough to see the joy and wonder in four eyes that had never before seen a lake or a dock or a rowboat or a fishing pole.

The boys squatted down to watch Ben bait the hooks. In a little while Jeffrey, who was holding a long cane pole with Retta's help, let out a squeal. The line was jumping up and down. Retta let him do most of the pulling, and up onto the dock flopped a mighty seven-inch bream.

No five-foot marlin ever caused such a ruckus. The little boys were beside themselves, and all the adults joined in the celebration. My only fear was that Jeffrey and Jamie might throw up from excitement!

The whole day must have been overwhelming for them: riding in the big bus (a first) with two dozen strangers; being greeted at the door of a bigger house than they'd ever dreamed existed; romping in the vast yard with two golden retrievers, playful but a little scary; making friends with a yellow-and-white tabby cat; and catching two slippery, shiny fish. (Jamie got one eventually, thank goodness. I'm afraid he had a bit of an impatient tantrum after Jeffrey's success.) They seemed to especially enjoy being turned loose at a picnic table that was laden with what must have seemed to them like a thousand choices, from chicken legs to lemon pie.

The Priests arrived just before lunch with Artie and Cliff and baby Louisa. My, those children have grown since I last saw them!

The four boys took to each other right away. Arthur had brought a soccer ball and one of those soft footballs. He kept them entertained when they finished eating.

The rest of us sat around sleepily in deck chairs after lunch, under an awning of spreading oak limbs, worn out with overeating.

After a while, when the ball games broke up, I saw Jeffrey run up and whisper something in Retta's ear. She spoke to Sidney, who then spoke to Ben. He shook his head, but the two adults and Jeff kept nodding their heads at him. Finally, Ben went out to where the bus was parked at the front gate, and came back with something in a cloth bag. It turned out to be an old-fashioned ukulele, a larger one than I had ever seen before.

Ben started tuning the strings, and people started waking up.

"Oh, good — some music!" said Cora.

No five-foot marlin ever caused such a rukus.

57

"Sing for us, Uncle Ben," said Jeffrey, shyly.

"What'll I sing, boy?"

"How 'bout 'Chicken in the Bread Tray'?"

"Aw, son. That ole thing?" (It sounded more like "thang," the way he said it.)

Jeffrey nodded and smiled. Ben twanged a few chords and began:

> "Chicken in the bread tray
> Scratchin' out dough.
> 'Granny, will your dog bite?'
> 'No, chile, no.' "

The way he imitated Granny's screechy voice made all the children laugh.

"Go on. Sing the rest," urged Jeffrey. And he did.

"Son," said Ben, when he finished that masterpiece of foolishness, "these are high-class folks. Let's give 'em somethin' a little better than that. How 'bout 'Little Brown Church in the Vale'?"

He started the song about the church in the wildwood, and in a minute the picnickers roused themselves and joined in on the chorus. The men had a good time rumbling, "Come, come, come, come. . . ."

This led to "Annie Laurie," "Old Black Joe," "My Old Kentucky Home," and "Aunt Dinah's Quilting Party."

"Ben," asked Sidney, "I wonder if you know an oldie called 'A Bulldog on the Bank'?"

"Sure! At least I used to. Let's do it together.

What I forget maybe you'll remember. You'd better be the dog. I've got the frog's voice."

So Sidney started off with, "Oh, the bulldog on the bank," and Ben came in with, "And the bullfrog in the pool." Then they both sang:

"The bulldog called the bullfrog
A green old water fool."

They stumbled through several verses, ending with the Pharaoh's daughter on the bank and Moses in the pool.

They made an odd pair: Sidney, tall, with silky gray hair and aristocratic features, wearing best-quality khaki slacks and an elegant striped cotton shirt; and Ben, short, with spiky, no-color hair, ruddy cheeks, bright eyes, his stocky figure clad in faded jeans and a T-shirt.

When the applause for their silly song had died down, Ben said, "Man, are we reachin' back! Let's come up a few decades." With that, he played some fast chords and started a jazzy melody: "I'm Alabamy Bound." By the time he launched into "Bye, Bye, Blackbird," he had everyone's feet twitching. Bill and Ann Nixon actually got up and did a few dance steps, which drew much applause.

When it was time to board the bus, the residents not only thanked Lucille for a wonderful day, but also thanked Ben for his musical contribution.

"You'll have to come out and get us to singing

at The Home some night, Mr. Stringfellow," said Cora. "And have supper. How about asking him out, Retta? And the little boys, too."

Retta turned and looked at Ben and the boys. They all nodded eagerly.

Soon after boarding the bus, Jeffrey and Jamie fell asleep, each clutching a dead fish in a paper bag. Ben's eyes were soon closed, too. I saw Retta and Sidney give each other a satisfied look. It had been a good day.

Chapter 4

Friends

October 31st

Mary Dunlap hasn't lived here long, but we feel that we've known her forever. She is the kind of person who fits right in, anywhere: friendly, funny, interested in people other than herself. (She has a high C.Q.) So I was sorry to learn that she had developed bad back problems and had to be in the infirmary, in traction. Instead of just sending her a get-well card, I wrote her a few lines:

> Mary, Mary's not contrary.
> She just has, alack,
> A dreadful bout of suffering
> In her sacro-iliac.
>
> Here's hoping she will soon throw off
> That halter (?), traction (?), sling (?)
> And start to do the Charleston,
> Or at least a Highland Fling!

While I was in a rhyming mood I wrote another verse inspired by the TV program "Firing Line." I watch it once in a while, if only to learn some new words from the host. But I can't help wishing he would sit up straight.

FIRING LINE ON THE BIAS
Bill Buckley sits so crookedly!
His stance, it is a sight.
But one good thing about it is
He's leaning to the right!

November 10th

My editor Evelyn Hogan and I have been busy this fall, keeping the mails and phone lines hot. She is an erudite lady, and I have agreed with most of her changes, but not all.

We argued for ten minutes one day (over long distance!) about the word "jackass." In the story, I had some of the residents talking about the kudzu vine — how it (and Yankees) are taking over the South. Somebody says, "I think the first kudzu in the United States was ordered from Japan, for a porch vine. Probably some jackass in Washington — probably in the Agriculture Department — was responsible for that."

Evelyn said, "I don't want you to use the word 'jackass' in that connection."

"Why in the world not?" I asked.

"Well, for one thing, my grandmother worked

in Washington, and she wasn't a jackass."

"I'm sure she wasn't," I countered, "but you know there are thousands of those critters up there."

"Now, Hattie. You're not a mean-spirited person. Let's not let any mean-spiritedness creep into this book."

So I had to give in, reluctantly. I still think that one little reference to a jackass, ordering a porch vine that would almost devour the South, could have been allowed.

But altogether, the editing has been going smoothly. Evelyn and I found we were kindred spirits in many ways, despite the age difference. I'm glad they assigned me to her.

December 15th

I haven't written in this journal in more than a month. I suppose the cause was partly being busy with my little book, partly a low-ness of spirit, due, no doubt, to the loss of a third great and good friend.

First there was Sarah Moorer, who died last year just when we had reached a lovely rapport. The next one was dear little Miss Minna McKenzie, the musician I enjoyed playing duets with. She slipped away with no fuss at all, which was just like her; but she left a big gap in our cultural life and in — what shall I call it? — the face we show to the world. We're not *quite* the well-bred, genteel group we were when she was a part of us.

I miss her terribly.

And then, a few weeks ago, we lost Angus McLeod. A quiet, gentle man. Not many people knew him well enough to say more than "Good morning" to him. But he and I started a friendship in The Home's "Country Store" one day, while licking ice cream cones. We found that we shared a great interest in things Scottish, because of our Highland ancestry.

People had thought him haughty, but it turned out to be shyness. Throat trouble had left his speech a little raspy, which he was very conscious of. Somehow I managed to put him at ease. (Asking questions was one way.) Anyway, we became fast friends.

Angus had a Cadillac that he took pride in, and he seemed to enjoy taking me to ride in it. We would sometimes take a picnic lunch and go to Middleton Gardens, or to the Isle of Palms.

I learned that Angus, a lifelong bachelor, was a Phi Beta Kappa, *summa cum laude* graduate of Davidson College — which I know is not easy to be — and that he had been a professor of English literature at that college for almost fifty years. I learned that he was an authority on William Wordsworth, my favorite poet. We had bashes, revels, feasts of quoting that gentleman's incomparable lyrical lines. If I couldn't dredge up a word or phrase, Angus, of course, could. Once I had the pleasure of catching *him* out, on the lines:

And much it grieved my heart to think
What Man has made of Man.

He was using the word "soul" instead of "heart."

The tongues at FairAcres, ever nimble, were just beginning to wag about Angus and me when he had a massive stroke. It happened on a Sunday, in the chapel. At the end of the service he couldn't get up from his seat. His color changed to that awful deathly pale shade we hate to see in this place. He was taken to the infirmary, and died an hour later.

I couldn't help being glad that he went quickly — that he would be spared the long, lingering half-life that many people have to endure. But oh! I miss him — and not only our literary confabs. He made me feel special as no one had since Sam died. A dear, quiet, lovable man.

So, I have been bereaved, Dear Diary, and have neglected you for a long time. I will try to improve. I will try to remember to take notes at the dinner table again, and transcribe them each evening. I (and you) have been missing too much "good stuff."

December 16th

A nurse in the infirmary told me this story about a man I'll call Mr. McMillan. In fact, I've heard several stories about this gentleman, a kind of aged Peck's Bad Boy, made even "badder" by senile dementia.

The nurse said she had to give him an "up-draft," or "peace-pipe" treatment, because he was having trouble breathing. She put the medicine in the pipe, put the pipe in his mouth, and turned around to do something else. When she turned back, he had stuck the pipe in his ear! The next day she put the medicine in the pipe, put it in his mouth, and watched to see that it stayed there. Quick as a flash he took the top off and drank the liquid out of it, "just like it was a shot of whiskey," she said.

One day when he was feeling frisky, and no one was watching, this same Mr. McMillan got into his wheelchair and rolled himself out into the hall, to see what he could find. There was the medicine cart with no one around. (The nurse was administering a dose inside a nearby room.) I can almost hear Mr. Mac saying, "Hot damn!" He opened every capsule, emptied every bottle of pills on the floor, mixed up all the liquids. He had a field day. I was not told what the nurse said when she came out and found the wreckage.

I hope there is a special, peaceful, elegant, happy corner in heaven for the nurses who toil patiently on earth in places like this!

Later

Looking at the date atop this page, I suddenly realize that there are only nine days till Christmas, and I haven't written Card Number One! Oh, dear. I haven't even *bought* a card. Maybe I will skip cards this year, and just call up a few people. What with the price of a decent card, and the postage, a call will cost very little more.

If I do that, I will be letting down another bar, taking the easy way, toppling another time-honored custom. That's not good. And yet, writing cards would mean opening my address book. That's something I hate to do, these days. At least every second name is crossed out. The crossings-out look angry, as if I resented having to do it — and I did. Even looking in passing at all those dear names — with addresses and phone numbers now belonging to someone else — always depresses me. I think I *will* skip cards this year. I'll rely on the numbers I keep in the back of my phone directory, and listen to a few friendly, familiar voices on long distance. (It will probably be after five o'clock, or on the weekend rates. My Scottish blood flows strong, even at Christmas.)

December 17th

During the sabbatical I took from journal-keeping, a number of interesting things happened that I don't want to fail to mention. Retta and Sidney invited Ben, Jeff, and Jamie to supper at The Home one night. (Our supper hour is early enough for young children, or for the earliest bird.)

As the little group entered our huge dining

room, I was close by and saw Jeffrey look around in wonder and then pull on Ben's sleeve. Ben leaned over, and I barely heard the little boy say timidly, "Mister Ben, all this room in *one* room?" Ben smiled and nodded, and held the small hand tighter.

Somebody (either Retta or Ben) had bought new winter coats for the boys, and with their freshly washed hair, enormous brown eyes, and shy good manners, they made a hit with our population.

Good things didn't stop there. Retta and I arranged for Jeffrey and Jamie to spend a weekend with the Priests at Kudzu Kottage. What a happy idea that was.

Oh, I have another update on Arthur: He has now been made head of the maintenance department of FairAcres! He has always been wonderful at solving problems around here, but before Louly Canfield recognized his dyslexia and painstakingly taught him to read, he couldn't get a driver's license or advance much on the job. We all rejoice over his promotion. He has a successful look about him these days.

The Davis boys were in seventh heaven when we left them that Saturday, and weary but happy when we came back for them on Sunday. The swing, slide, and sandbox that Arthur had made had been put to joyful use.

Dollie said all the children had gotten along well. "But," she reported, "Jamie must learn to watch his language!"

"What in the world happened?" I asked.

"Well, he stumped his toe on a root, and I heard him say, 'Dod dammit!' Then twice later he used bad four-letter words."

"Oh, dear! I'm afraid Mrs. Hawkins may be to blame," said Retta.

"Who's Mrs. Hawkins?" asked Dollie.

"She's their grandmother," explained Retta, "but she seems to have an alcohol problem and is all too happy when Ben or Sidney or I take the boys off her hands for a while. Did Jeffrey do any bad talking?"

"He did once, but he seems to know better," Dollie said. "He even scolded Jamie and threatened to tell their mama."

Retta looked at me and shook her head. "I thought I heard one or two bad words at the picnic," she said, "when a fish would let go of the bait — but I decided my ears must have been fooling me."

"Oh, dear!" I said, but we had to laugh. The little profane angels!

Retta and I are going to a mall near Charleston tomorrow to buy Christmas gifts for the boys, and something for Mr. Stringfellow. I'm hoping to find a ukulele or child-sized guitar for Jeff; he seems particularly interested in Ben's music. I hope we can find something to help use up Jamie's seemingly inexhaustible supply of energy.

We were delighted to learn that Arthur and

Dollie have invited Ben and the whole Davis family to have Christmas dinner at Kudzu Kottage. Though the Priests were nice enough to invite the mother and grandmother, Mrs. Davis has to work that day and Mrs. Hawkins refused the invitation. She'll probably enjoy her liquid refreshments in peace and quiet.

Let's see. What else has happened? . . . Oh, yes. There was a fashion show, put on by The Village Couturier, a nice dress shop in Drayton. The manager, Mr. Grant, arranged to rent our dining room (one of the largest rooms in town) for an evening, with the understanding that all residents could attend, free. Many ladies and two men took advantage, joining the large crowd of people from town.

Just to be nice (I suppose), Mr. Grant asked two of our ladies — good customers of his — to be *in* the show. That was a mistake. Now, there are several women among our FairAcres population who would have made good models — brisk and smiling — but the two he honored were shaky and scared. Not only that, but they both wore high heels — I don't know whose idea that was. Both of them stumbled as they came down the steps from the stage. Somebody caught them. They weren't hurt, thank goodness, but I could have cried. They were so embarrassed.

The brightest spot of the evening — to us — was completely unplanned. Our dining room is just a short corridor away from the infirmary.

70

Vera Wescott, a walk-around patient there who has a number of very loose screws, managed to slip by the nurses' desk and came wandering into the fashion show in her hideous plum-colored bathrobe and cotton scuffs. She found a chair down near the front, and proceeded to bring life to the occasion.

As Vera seated herself, one of The Home's models happened to be on the stage, making an amateurish, unsteady pivot.

"Watch her teeterin' on those high heels!" exclaimed Vera in her very carrying voice. "At her age she oughta be home in bed," she continued, punching her neighbor with her elbow.

The next model was young, but her knees weren't pretty enough (whose are?) for the twenty-two-inch skirt she was showing. Vera came out with a song I hadn't heard in sixty years:

> Oh, they're wearin' them higher
>   in Ha-wa-ya,
> Goin' up, goin' up every day!

The crowd loved it, so Vera kept up her remarks, almost drowning out poor Mr. Grant's gentlemanly commentary.

He managed to get in a line about hats coming back in. "You will see," he said, "that our next model's outfit — perfect for church or a small tea party — is complete with a chic chapeau."

The dress was stylish and becoming, but the

hat was awkward looking. The crown came down to the girl's eyebrows.

"That's a mighty po' chapeau, if you ask me," said Vera, shaking her head. "All right to feed the chickens in, maybe."

Somebody clapped, which was all the encouragement Vera needed.

"Tsk, tsk!" Vera exclaimed when the next young model came in wearing a tight bathing suit. "Child, does your mother know where you are? Dressed like that? *Un*dressed like that?"

Things were getting out of hand, now, and I saw someone head down the hall toward the infirmary to summon help. The next model appeared on the stage in an elaborate evening dress of shimmering material, covered with sequins and pearls. Vera shook her head and said, "Ummm, *ummm.* Where's she gonna wear that in *this* town? To the pool hall?"

Just then two aides from the infirmary arrived and insisted on escorting Mrs. Wescott back to her room, much against her wishes. A few people clapped as she was led out. I'm sure Mr. Grant was ready to sue somebody. At the very least, I expect it will be a long time before he rents our dining room again!

December 18th

When I heard last week that there would be a rendition of Handel's *Messiah* at a local church tonight, by a group from Charleston, I asked Mr.

Detwiler if The Home could take some of us in the small bus to hear it. He readily agreed, and he and his wife went with us.

He has a great fondness for classical music. Maybe it soothes his soul, after running into so much contrariness during the week.

The music was beautiful and stirring, but I'll tell you something, Dear Diary: I thought Herr Handel missed about ten good stopping places. It went on and on. Do you suppose George Frideric got paid by the stave, or the canto, or something?

I think the choruses are about a hundred and fifty hallelujahs too long. That's blasphemy, I know; but my bottom is poorly fleshed these days, and the church seat was not exactly downy. I saw some wriggling in some other pews, too, after about ten dozen "King of Kings" and "Lord of Lords."

I don't mean to be sacrilegious, but I think even the finest of worshipful music can be overdone. We have condensed books for the hard-of-seeing; why not condensed oratorios for the hard-of-sitting?

Forgive me, George Frideric Handel, wherever you are. I like many of your majestic offerings, but *Messiah* is a little hard for me to Handle. (Oo-oo-oo, that's terrible, Hattie. You're not only blasphemous tonight, you're corny.)

December 19th

I listened to Paul and Curtis this afternoon, unbeknownst to them. They weren't quite as full of beans as usual. I'm afraid my "merry men" are ailing. They sat quietly for a while, watching the evening shadows gather, and then Paul said, "I heard something pretty good at the barber shop today. Somebody said, 'Don't tell an Englishman a joke on Saturday night. He might start laughing in church the next morning.' "

It took Curtis a minute to catch on. He finally laughed and said, "I get it. The Limeys are a little slow on the uptake . . . like me, today. Well, I remember one about a bunch of old men sitting around on the porch of a country store in North Carolina on a June day a long time ago, listenin' to a fellow on the radio sayin' that D-Day and the invasion of Normandy had begun.

"One man looked at the lovely blue sky and white clouds, and said, 'Well, they sure picked a good day for it!' "

December 20th

There's so much that's ironic about old age. For example: Couples who finally have a little financial ease, and are too old to enjoy it. I know three couples who tell me that they looked forward so much to the time when they would have the money and leisure to travel. Now they have both, but not the physical strength to do it. That's sad.

When my children ask me why I don't take trips — even go abroad — I tell them I couldn't enjoy the scenery. I'd be too busy looking for a restroom.

Incidentally, I wonder if those quaint rooms (with chain pulls) in old English hotels are still called Water Closets?

My daughter, Nancy, is picking me up tomorrow to spend the holidays with her family. It will be wonderful to be with the children for Christmas. I rejoice that we have an easygoing relationship: I take it easy, and I let them do all the going!

January 2nd

Well, I feel "home" again, in my cozy apartment at The Home. The holidays were delightful, but somewhat exhausting. I did not take it quite as easy as I planned, but I enjoyed seeing family and a number of "auld acquaintance" who have managed to ring in another New Year with fortitude and good grace. Nancy arranged lunch for several old cronies and me during the week after Christmas. That was my best present.

One of my friends told me a story about a lady in the infirmary of another retirement home — not ours. The lady needed the bedpan, and she rang her bell, but nobody came. She rang and rang, but it seems the nurses were busy with an emergency.

Anyway this lady finally picked up the phone on the table by her bed and called 911. She soon had attention.

I'm not recommending such a practice, but she was desperate — and it worked!

Chapter 5

Where There's Smoke . . .

January 8th

Coming out of church service at the chapel this morning I found myself walking with Marcia Coleman. It was plain to see that she was out of sorts.

Our chaplain had taken as his text that great verse from Philippians: "I have learned, in whatever state I am, therewith to be content." His exegesis had been quite good, I thought — but it apparently had not assuaged whatever was vexing Marcia.

"What's the matter?" I asked her.

"At least half a dozen things," she said. "I find it hard to be real content with my state when I've got an ingrown toenail, and a blister on my hand from trying to transplant a bush." (Marcia has one of the cottages behind The Home, with a lovely garden she has developed.) "Besides that, I think I'm coming down with cystitis, and I'm overdrawn at the bank. And there's something else that's driving me nuts. I had to get out of the house a while, it was making me so nervous. To tell you the truth, that's why I went to church."

"What's wrong at your house?"

"There's a noise — a cheeping noise. I know there's a tiny bird loose in my house, and I can't find it because my eyes are so bad these days. That little, 'cheep . . . cheep,' is about to drive me crazy! I guess I'll have to open the doors and chase it out with a broom — if I can *find* the pesky thing."

This attitude was surprising, coming from Marcia, a bird lover. She *must* be upset, I thought.

"Tell you what," I suggested, "let's go by the maintenance office. Even on Sunday I think someone might be there who could help you capture that bird."

Sure enough, a young fellow named Aaron was on duty and said he'd be glad to go with us and see what he could do.

We entered Marcia's living room. She said, "Be still, and listen. You'll hear the sound in a minute."

Sure enough, it came — a shrill "cheep." I started looking around for a bird, but Aaron didn't. He walked straight to the hallway that led to Marcia's bedroom and reached up to a gadget on the wall.

"Ma'am, it's your smoke alarm," he announced. "When the battery's getting low, it beeps. I'll go get a new battery for you, and be right back."

When he left, Marcia and I fell on each other, laughing.

"I feel so *silly*," she said. "I've been swatting around the walls with a broom, and cussing out a poor little nonexistent bird! How stupid can you get?"

We laughed and laughed, and I could tell that it did her good. Norman Cousins was right. Laughter *is* the best cure for everything.

Maybe Chaplain Brewer could take as another text the words from Proverbs: "A merry heart doeth good like a medicine."

January 10th

I came upon Sidney Metcalf in our small post office today. He was reading a letter, and frowning.

Seeing me, he said, "Hattie, I need to talk to you. Could we go out on the terrace for a minute?"

Now, Sidney is a smart man. He realized the past few months that Retta was not to be won quickly; so I noticed that he had eased up, and stopped pushing her. He does good thinking, though — like discovering pleasant places for the two of them to go to lunch after doing their Meals-on-Wheels stint. Sometimes they go to Charleston, sometimes across the picturesque

Cooper River bridge to a seafood restaurant in Mt. Pleasant.

They went to see some of the daytime performances at The Spoleto Festival, and on a warm, bright day recently they took a jaunt to Brookgreen Gardens, up near Georgetown.

Retta came back from that excursion all aglow. "Hattie," she reported, "that's one of the most fascinating places I've ever seen! You must go there."

"I've been there, honey child. Many times. I'm descended from the first owners of that plantation."

"You *are?* Why didn't you tell me?"

"I don't go around bragging on my ancestors. Anyway, it's just a collateral descent, not a direct one. What has always interested me," I went on, "is that Aaron Burr's daughter, Theodosia, lived there before her sad disappearance."

"Well," said Retta, "there's certainly an air about the place. Just walking down the avenue, between those humongous oaks, was romantic enough — but, oh, that sculpture we came upon! I nearly lost my mind. Sidney knows a lot about art. I don't mean he shows off about it; but he was able to explain to me certain differences in styles of sculpture. So *many* famous artists have works displayed there. I oohed and aahed like a country-come-to-town hick."

And I'll bet he loved it, I thought. They are so well suited. I wonder if Retta's beginning to realize that? I had been discouraged when she told

80

me, before the holidays, that she hoped he wouldn't get too serious.

"I've had one husband. That's enough. Getting married again is not on my agenda," she had said with too much conviction to suit me.

When Sidney and I found seats in the sunshine, he unfolded the letter again.

"This is from my son, Gerald. In some way — I wonder how — he has learned that I am seriously courting a lady here at The Home. He doesn't actually say so, but I can tell that he is worried."

"Why?" I asked. "Isn't he interested in your happiness?"

"Oh, I'm sure he is." He tried to smile. "Maybe he and his sisters think I'm senile and liable to be 'taken in' by the wrong kind of person." He made a face. "Think of it. Retta! The wrong kind of person!"

"Maybe if they met her —" I began to suggest.

"That's just it," he interrupted. "He and Sue and Thelma are coming here — this Sunday! — on a kind of 'tour of inspection,' though, of course, he doesn't call it that. Don't you know Retta will hate it? Such a private person. . . . Hattie, will you help me? She might even refuse to meet them. Will you persuade her to at least have one meal with them — Sunday dinner? Will you try?"

He looked so distraught that I could only say yes to the dear man, but I wondered if I could

81

follow through . . . knowing Retta.

"And please, Hattie, sit at the table with us on Sunday. I shall need reinforcements!"

Oh, dear. *The course of true love never did run smooth,* as the Bard said. I suppose it's especially rough when you're seventy-five and have complications like a family from a former life.

I forgot to put in, above, that Sidney said his children were inordinately fond of their mother's memory. She had been an indulgent, loving parent.

"Almost too much so," he said. "She spoiled them."

I suppose they find it hard to think of anyone — *anyone* — replacing her in their father's affections.

Something else has occurred to me. It's a mean thought. I understand that Sidney has a rather princely share of this world's goods — a share that his children may not be keen to split, later, with a stepmother. I'm being blunt, but that can well be a factor in such cases.

January 12th

When I saw Retta today, I broached the subject of the impending visit of Sidney's children. She said very matter-of-factly that she wouldn't think of meeting them.

"That would make it too pointed a matter," she stated — or words to that effect.

My rather weak rejoinder was that *not* meeting

them might be even more pointed (although I wasn't really sure what I meant by that).

January 15th

I am exhausted from the effort, Dear Diary, but I must tell you about today's "family dinner" with Sidney's offspring. We all tried to be pleasant and attractive, but there was a strained feeling — a lack of spontaneous congeniality. I felt sorry for Retta. Sidney's progeny had obviously caught the sound of wedding bells, and they were not pleased about it. You could tell they were here to learn all they could about a certain widow named Henrietta Gooding.

Yesterday, in desperation, I had told Retta that Sidney, my old and valued friend, had made me promise that I would have my old and valued friend — her — there, at that dinner. (In my plight, I stretched the truth a little.)

"Oh, all right," she said, reluctantly. "Since your *honor* is at stake," she added with a sly smile and a sigh. "But I'm not looking forward to the rendezvous one bit."

Today we all met in the library, as arranged. I was impressed by the good looks of Sidney's children; but you could have cut the chilliness with a knife.

Soon after we took our seats in the dining room, the youngest child, Sue, said, "That's a lovely dress, Mrs. Gooding. Did you find it in Charleston?"

"No. I haven't been here long enough to learn about the area shops. I order most of my clothes from New York."

"Do you like living here?" asked Gerald.

"Well, it takes a little getting used to. It's an institution, after all. But a number of nice people, including Mrs. McNair and your father, have gone all out to help me make the transition. I'm grateful to them." She smiled at Sidney and me. The children looked at each other.

We ate in silence for a time.

"Do you have children?" inquired Thelma.

"No. Unfortunately, my only child died at age six. Do you have children?"

"Oh, yes!" said Thelma. "We've given Daddy seven 'grands.' "

She made this sound like a phenomenal accomplishment. I'm being catty, but I was beginning to dislike this situation. I didn't like the way they were looking at my friend. I wanted to say, *She hasn't encouraged him. Just the opposite, in fact.*

Well, let me skip to the good part of the conversation.

Sidney asked Gerald, "How's business, son?"

"Pretty good, Dad, and showing signs of getting better. I think I might have a chance of signing a contract soon with Konnmore."

"Really? With Konnmore?"

"The same. One of the ten biggest corporations in the South. You know about it, don't you?" Gerald asked rather self-importantly, looking in Retta's direction.

Sidney and Retta exchanged an amused look, and Sidney nodded to his son. "Oh, yes. I know a little more about it . . . now. Retta's grandfather, Lawrence Konn, started that company."

"He *did?*" Gerald's expression was a sight to see.

"And Retta is one of the principal stockholders," Sidney went on. "I've heard her fussing about having to go to Charlotte for directors' meetings."

There were a few long seconds, and then Sue said, "I suppose it would get to be a bore. Personally, I wouldn't mind being bored that way."

We finished our dessert quietly, and parted company rather coolly. It was an interesting occasion, to say the least. Overtones and undertones . . . an American family drama. I wonder what the *denouement* will be.

January 17th

Pearl's door was open. As I passed her room in the infirmary, she called out, "Who's that?" I backed up and said, "It's Hattie."

"Come in, Hattie, please, and help me find it."

"Find what?" I asked as I stepped through her door.

"You know. What we're lookin' for."

I said, "What are you looking for?"

"You know," Pearl said, impatiently, "the thing we want to find."

85

Sidney's progeny had obviously caught the sound of wedding bells, and they were not pleased about it.

"But I don't know what we want to find," I replied.

"Then why are we lookin' for it?"

Oh, dear.

January 18th

Louly Canfield has a toaster in her room. It's an old one, and this morning it failed to send the slices popping up. Instead, it burnt the toast and made enough smoke to set off the fire alarm.

In an amazingly short time four firefighters from the Drayton Fire Department were on the scene, taking care of the tiny conflagration. What impressed Louly most were the good looks of the young men who showed up in her kitchenette.

"I declare! If I'd known what handsome firemen this town had, I'd have burnt my toast sooner!"

The excitement reminded me of the last time we had a serious fire drill. It was held fairly late in the evening, and at the shrill sound, we all came tumbling out of our rooms in various kinds of odd raiment, and everyone gathered on the front porch and terrace, as we had instructions to do — everyone, that is, except for Dr. Browning.

After several minutes had passed and he hadn't appeared, Cora decided to go after him. She ran down his hall and banged on that very proper gentleman's door. (He's a retired Presbyterian minister.)

"Doctor Browning! Doctor Browning! Come out! It's a fire drill!"

"I know," came the dignified voice. "I know, madam, and I'm coming." He opened the door a crack. "I will be there shortly, madam, but I will burn to a crisp before I come out without my trousers on."

"Right! Yes, sir. Right," said Cora, slinking away.

Chapter 6

Over What Hill?

January 19th

I love my morning paper, but not what its inky-ness does to my hands and to my sofa and to whatever I have on. I can't do anything about it except to make up a rhyme:

> The ink that coats my *Courier*
> Is thick as morning dews.
> I have to put an apron on
> To read the morning news!

January 20th

A new resident, Virginia Phillips, swears this happened. Her friend's aged mother, not in the best of mental states, was being "prepped" for an operation.

When the daughter arrived, the nurse said, "We're having a time with your mother. She won't let us take out her false teeth. I've been trying for ten minutes. She keeps biting me!"

"No wonder," said the daughter, laughing. "Those are *her* teeth, not dentures!"

January 22nd

This has been a quiet Sunday of musings.

Thomas Jefferson, in his old age, wrote: "There is a ripeness of time for death . . . when it is reasonable we should drop off, and make room for another growth. When we have lived our generation out, we should not wish to encroach on another."

He's right, I suppose. (He usually was.) But . . . who can know exactly when that "ripeness of time" has arrived? Most of us hang on to life, clutching. In some cases I wonder why. Why cling to the kind of condition Charles Kingsley was describing in *The Water Babies*:

When all the world is old, lad,
And all the trees are brown,
And all the sport is stale, lad,
And all the wheels run down. . . .

And yet . . . and yet . . . If Grandma Moses had shuffled off at threescore and ten, we would have missed her great contribution to American art. If Goethe had "given up the ghost" before his eighty-second year, we would not have *Faust: Part II*. If Michelangelo had not lived and worked until his late seventies, we would have been deprived of magnificent sculptures, including *The Crucifixion of St. Peter.*

Were all those gifted people "over the hill"? I don't think so! In fact, after thinking it over, I say to Mr. Jefferson: Times have changed somewhat since your day, sir. There are things to keep us, not just alive, but thriving longer as beings on this earth. Nowadays, everything is not downhill after we join the AARP.

Yes, there's sadness and much loss, Mr. Kingsley, when all the wheels run down; but as Tennyson's Ulysses said, something abides. I will hold that thought.

January 24th

A resident of our infirmary — someone who has been there since long before the name was changed to the Health Care Center — has always been quiet and ladylike. But this afternoon something infuriated her, and she came out with a stream of wicked profanity. A shocked witness (who was recounting the event before supper tonight) recovered sufficiently to ask her where and when she had learned those words. To which the lady replied airily, "Oh, I've known them a long time, but just never had a good chance to use them before."

Speaking of words, I used one that I regret in a letter I wrote and mailed yesterday.

At two o'clock this morning I sat up in bed, thinking: It's insightful, not in*cite*ful! The man I was writing to didn't want to incite anything! I was trying to compliment him on his discernment, and I made a fool of myself.

Oh, dear. It serves me right for trying to be smarty-fied. Why didn't I just say, "your very sensible remarks"?

I love words, and I like to throw in a rare one occasionally; but I'd better consult Mr. Webster a little more than I've been doing lately. I've had a love affair with the English language since the fifth grade, when I began to appreciate the dictionary. Our language is so satisfying in its plenitude; and it grieves me when I come out with an egregiously wrong word when we have been furnished with a right word for *everything*.

It's no wonder words, letters of the alphabet, and even punctuation marks have been dancing in my head day and night lately. My editor and I have been going over the final proofs of my book, mailing chapters back and forth. We want to find *all* the errors — perhaps an impossible goal — but we both have old-fashioned standards about typographical errors and are working hard to catch them before they jump off the page of the printed book at us!

January 26th

We have a kind of sew-around circle that meets twice a month in somebody's apartment or in one of the parlors. We teach each other different kinds of knitting or crochet stitches, and different ways of making bibs, aprons, hand towels, etc., to sell in The Home's craft shop. The proceeds go to charity.

What I think we look forward to, more than learning new tricks in handiwork, is the talking, the tale-telling, the reminiscences that are sometimes a little bit sad, but more often are killingly funny.

Today Tilly told about the time she went to a doctor's office in Orangeburg. She and about ten other people had been sitting for more than two hours when the doctor's nurse came into the waiting room and said, "The doctor has been detained at the hospital on an emergency. He won't get here for hours. You people might as well go home."

Everyone got up to leave except the country woman who had been sitting beside Tilly.

"Aren't you coming?" asked Tilly.

"No, ma'am. Not me. I'm not leavin'. I come too far. And besides, I took a bath this mornin'!"

After we had whooped over that and caught our breath, Cora piped up.

"My tale is not as funny as that. It's about my first job. I had just finished business school, and answered a 'Wanted: Stenographer' ad. The Depression was in full swing. I was just eighteen, and scared. A big, burly man interviewed me, and I know I was shaking.

"Finally, he said, 'Well, I'll tell you what, missy.

We'll start you off at $15.00 a week, and see how much water you draw.' "

Cora said she wondered what in the world he meant. But she needed the job so badly, she decided to take it, even if she had to go to a well and draw water. She was apprehensive, but later she learned it was just an expression used by people who worked around boats a lot. Within a few weeks, she received a munificent raise, to $18.00 a week, so she knew she must be drawing a fair amount of water.

Myra, who has lived here twelve years, told us about a woman named Edith who lived and died here before most of us came. It seems that Edith liked to celebrate the end of the day (or maybe just getting through another day!) with a glass of something stronger than The Home's apple juice. And why not? Such a practice is advocated by many doctors, old and young. The young ones, especially (who act as if they know everything about aging), seem to push for "toddies" for the elderly.

Anyway, Edith, having been raised strictly, as a preacher's daughter, felt that she must keep her afternoon tippling *sub rosa*. One day, however, she began having trouble with the plumbing in her apartment. She was very reluctant about calling maintenance, which, Myra explained, was understandable after the plumber found a bottle of Ancient Age bourbon and two bottles of wine in the tank of her "john." It seems that the labels had soaked off of the

Sidney has a cold, and Retta insisted that he not get out in the rainy weather and deliver meals today.

bottles and had stopped up the pipe!

Myra said that Edith went around with her eyes averted for days. No one ever learned whether or not Edith found another hiding place.

February 1st

Sidney has a cold, and Retta insisted that he not get out in the rainy weather and deliver meals today. She called me about ten o'clock this morning and asked me to bundle up and go with her, which I did.

She took Sidney's car and his big insulated chest.

I enjoyed meeting some of the people Retta has been telling me about, but we didn't tarry long enough to visit because of the inclement weather. She and I had a nice visit, however, driving from place to place; but she refused to talk about Sidney's children.

"I choose not to dwell on them," she declared. "I don't want them to affect my friendship with their father for good or ill. When Sidney apologized for their intrusiveness, I told him that I enjoy his company and I prefer not to concern myself with their curiosity."

She claims to have dismissed the whole event, and I suppose I'm just glad it didn't make her dismiss Sidney. Retta has always been very level-headed.

February 2nd

Trudy is ninety-three years old, and she apparently thinks that ninety-plus years give her a special license to speak her mind. We do pet her and laugh at her — maybe too much. She can say embarrassing things right in front of the person she's talking about!

Today, waiting in line for lunch, she said, "I don't see why God takes away so many men, and leaves so many widows. It's just not right." She shook her head, and a henna-colored wave moved from over one eye to the center of her forehead. She wears a wig, and sometimes it gets a little askew, especially if she gets vehement about something.

"That new woman — Retta What's-Her-Name —"

I looked around, but Retta was not in the line, thank goodness.

"— she's got it made. A dead husband and a boy friend! *And* I hear she's playing hard-to-get. She'd better watch out. Too many waitin' in the wings. Lordy me! If I had charge of that man's future, I'd turn to that lined-up bunch of ladies and say, 'Take a number, and sit down.' "

February 6th

Ethel was fussing today about her children's occupations.

"You'd think that I, with three sons, could have

97

a doctor, a lawyer, and a plumber. But, no! I don't have any of those. All three of them are in the real estate business. They don't do me a bit of good. I don't have any property to sell, and I'm not planning to buy any. . . . I might need a little place in Heaven, but I'm pretty sure they don't have any listings there. They haven't studied the territory enough!"

February 15th

A man was giving a very serious talk in the library on Alzheimer's, which (to tell you the truth) seemed to me to be a rather wasted effort. There is no way to ward off that dread disease, and no one who has it would have sense enough to know it or to gain anything from a lecture about it.

Anyway, one of our number — one of the many of us who are turning flaky — came in, late, and sat in the back. After about five minutes of listening to the speaker's droning erudition, she called out, "For Lord's sake, somebody change the channel!"

March 1st

It's downright embarrassing the way some songs make me cry these days. I know it's a sign of the weakness of old age. I simply can't staunch the flow of tears when I hear something like I did tonight, in an old Western movie:

We beat the drum slowly
and played the fife lowly.
We wept in our grief as we bore him along.
For we loved the young cowboy,
so brave and so handsome.
We loved that young cowboy,
altho' he'd done wrong.

There are numerous other songs that get to me, such as: "None But the Lonely Heart (can know my sadness)"; the plaintive melody now called "Goin' Home," from Dvořák's *New World* Symphony (it was played at my father's funeral); Brahms's sweet "Lullaby"; "Swing Low, Sweet Chariot (comin' for to carry me home)"; and so many others.

Many hymns get to me, especially the patriotic ones we sing near the Fourth of July. The Christmas hymns do me in — probably because they take me back to happy childhood times.

Tears even come with a few fine hymns that are not at all sad: "Joyful, Joyful, We Adore Thee" and "A Mighty Fortress Is Our God." I suppose it's because they're beautiful and meaningful, and because I've been singing them (after a fashion) since I was three feet high, and was safely surrounded by loved ones in the pew.

Speaking of singing, music was really in the air today. March has come in like a lamb, and the birds were heralding spring with their songs this afternoon. Then tonight after supper, two ladies sang some pleasing duets. Their accompanist did a nice job, too. It made me wistful for my piano duets with dear Miss Minna. Rest her soul.

Rose Hibben's sense of humor rescued me from melancholy, however. She turned to me at the end of the program and declared, "I wish I could sing, but I sound like a frog. I remember when my Mary was sick, when she was about three years old. I said, 'Honey, would you like mama to rock you and sing to you?' After a minute, Mary said, 'Just rock.' Out of the mouths of babes!" And we had a good chuckle to exit on.

March 15th

On the Ides of March, of all days! I thought it would never come, but at last it did: the lovely day in early spring when I held my creation in my hands! Next to having a first baby, I suppose there's nothing quite like "having" your first book. Having it at such a great age just seemed to make it more of a lovely miracle.

I received an overnight package with three copies and a letter from my publisher explaining that these were "advance" copies and that shipments would begin to go out in a day or two to bookstores. The local bookstore in Drayton and our Library Committee are planning a party here as soon as books are in hand.

I am charmed with the book's jacket, which pictures a behatted old lady not unlike yours truly. In an eye-catching way, it conjures up a

"Poor Old Soul" embarking on the last phase of her life. Perfect.

March 17th

A call from Atlanta today confirmed that books will be "on the shelves" next week, and the autograph party here is set for a week from Sunday. Retta and I toasted the luck of the Irish and my publishing "luck" today when she came for a glass of sherry. I just had to share my excitement and a sneak peek at the collection of my jottings with someone. Who better than my dear friend from college days, the one who originally inspired me to put my thoughts on paper!

I also had the chance to catch up on news of Sidney's now extremely attentive children. Since the awkward Sunday dinner and Sidney's expression of thanks for my help, I had not heard any more. I certainly didn't want to pry.

But Retta seems undisturbed by it all. She told me that she did not enjoy the attention (inquisitiveness, if you ask me) that prompted the "family dinner" after the holidays, but that she was happy that all three children were now keeping in much better touch with their father. Sue has even invited Sidney to spend a month with them at the beach this summer. In the past he has been asked for only a weekend. He, of course, is thoroughly delighted at the idea of seeing his family for such an extended time.

Meanwhile, the deliveries for Meals on Wheels

continue, and Retta has promised to go on another golf outing next week if the lovely weather holds.

March 27th

People here at The Home have been wonderful about my book. There seems to be no jealousy — just pleasure and excitement about my accomplishment. I had some qualms about residents reading the book and seeing resemblances. I put a notice in our weekly paper, *Family Affairs*, begging them not to do that. I asked them to remember that the book is fiction, and that in fiction there is often much exaggeration.

Yesterday afternoon the Library Committee gave an autograph party for me, with all proceeds going for new large-print books for our collection. All my children came to the party! I said to the one who lives in North Carolina, "Son, there's no use for you to come that long way just to see some old people lined up to buy a little-bitty book." But he came, and thanks to a camera-nut friend, I should have some good pictures of the children, of me, and of all my dear, loyal "fellow inmates" — who bought one hundred and *fifty* books! Bless their hearts!

Chapter 7

Nourishment

March 29th

Once in a while Retta talks about other people on her Meals-on-Wheels route besides Mr. Stringfellow and his small neighbors. Tonight she mentioned Mr. and Mrs. Simpson, who live about a mile out of town.

"Their house is very modest, but so neat, and Hattie, you should see the yard! They have beautiful daffodils and azaleas blooming now, and the whole yard looks ready to burst into a spring flourish.

"They have so many rose bushes and flower beds with what look like old-fashioned flowers. Though you couldn't prove it by me — a horticulturist I'm not. But I can appreciate their hard work, and the way they have bordered the beds with shells. I don't know how in the world they do it, either. She is practically blind, and Mr. Simpson has crippling arthritis.

"I said something one day about his size. He's enormous, even in his bent-over state. He grinned and said, 'Ma'am, you shoulda seen my daddy. That was a *man*. He was so strong and worked so hard that Mr. Mayfield — him that owned the sawmill where my daddy worked — gave him two men's rations and paid him two men's wages!'

" 'My goodness!' I said. 'He must've been quite a man! Mr. Simpson, I'm curious. What did your father eat?'

"He scratched his head, looked up at the sky, and after a while, he said, 'Well, ma'am, I think he mostly et fatback, and collard greens, and turnips, and yams, and cowpeas, and cornbread.'

"His wife said, 'Don't forgit the blackstrap molasses on that cornbread!'

"I asked them if cowpeas and black-eyed peas were the same thing.

" 'The same very thing,' said Mr. Simpson. 'I don't know how come they got the name of cowpeas, but that's what we call 'em.'

"So there you have it, Hattie. A diet to produce giants. . . . Can't you just see it written up in the slick magazines: Greens for the Gods! Cornpones Crawling with Calories, but Guaranteed to Put Hair on Your Chest and Muscles on Your Muscles!"

I laughed, but after Retta left my apartment I kept thinking: There's some meat in that idea — literally! Men like Mr. Simpson's father did yeoman's work. What nourished them must have been the right thing. We could learn from it.

Simple, inexpensive, down-to-earth food. No thought of fat content or calories or cholesterol. They just ate heartily and worked it off.

I was about to forget to put this in: Retta said she asked Mr. S. how old his father was when he died.

"Ninety-one," he told her, "and he worked at the sawmill till he was seventy-nine."

March 30th

Nancy Bissell is a new resident who is having a little difficulty getting adjusted. She had lived in Columbia for years, enjoying the amenities of a university town: on-the-road Broadway plays, lectures, concerts, etc. Cultural life in Drayton doesn't *quite* measure up.

Anyway, she made such a nice "fuss" over me at the autograph party and said she hoped we could visit soon, so I went to call on her today. She told me that she was standing in the waiting line for lunch yesterday, feeling a little homesick among strangers, when the lady in front of her turned and with no preamble said, "You must smile a lot to have all those wrinkles in your cheeks." Nancy said she was a bit nonplussed, and her homesickness was not at all alleviated. (No wonder!)

She seemed a little blue, so I asked her to go with Retta and me to a special program in the chapel tonight after supper. I had heard that a professor of English literature from the state university, with a good reputation as a speaker, was to give a talk on "Poetry and Aging." Nancy said she might come; she wasn't sure. I started to remind her that each newcomer — as well as the welcoming community — must put forth some effort toward a happy adjustment. She did not show up tonight, but I'll ask her to something again.

Retta and I had not been seated for five minutes when — surprise — Mr. Sidney Metcalf asked if he could join us. Of course, we made room.

Fortunately I took my tape recorder with me as Dr. Honeywell gave us the best forty minutes I've spent in many a day. He was a tonic for all of us. Here are some of the highlights.

He said, "I will try to get serious in a few minutes; but first let me quote to you some silly rhymes that have delighted me, all by that silly-rhymes master, Ogden Nash:

> There was an old man of Calcutta
> Who coated his tonsils with butta,
> Thus converting his snore
> From a thunderous roar
> To a soft, oleaginous mutta.

And this one:

> Senescence begins
> And middle age ends
> The day your descendants
> Outnumber your friends.

"That last one is not so funny, is it, friends?" he commented. "I know that most of you are in your seventies or eighties, so you will relate to a poem by Longfellow called 'Nature.' In the first lines, it deals with children reluctant to leave their toys to go to bed; then it says:

> So Nature deals with us, and takes away
>   Our playthings one by one, and by the hand
>   Leads us to rest so gently, that we go
> Scarce knowing if we wish to go or stay,
>   Being too full of sleep to understand
>   How far the unknown transcends the
> what we know.

"Isn't that wonderful?" asked our speaker. "Who says Longfellow is obsolete? I'm sixty-five, and those lines are comforting to me.

"Then there are some stirring words by an aging Ralph Waldo Emerson:

> As the bird trims her to the gale
> I trim myself to the storm of time,
> I man the rudder, reef the sail,
> Obey the voice at eve obeyed at prime:
> 'Lowly faithful, banish fear,
> Right onward drive unharmed;
> The port, well worth the cruise, is near,
> And every wave is charmed.'

"I especially like the line: 'The port, well worth the cruise, is near.'

"Also, we have the beautiful, upbeat thoughts that Robert Louis Stevenson put into his rhyme called 'Requiem':

Under the wide and starry sky
Dig the grave and let me lie.
Glad did I live and gladly die,
And I laid me down with a will. . . .

This be the verse you grave for me:
Here he lies where he longed to be;
Home is the sailor, home from sea,
And the hunter home from the hill.

"I'm sure you all have heard the first two lines of a poem by William Cowper:

God moves in a mysterious way,
    His wonders to perform; . . . .

But I like a verse farther down in that poem:

Ye fearful saints fresh courage take,
    The clouds ye so much dread
Are big with mercy, and shall break
    In blessings on your head.

"And then," Dr. Honeywell continued, "there is Alfred Tennyson, who begged that there be no moaning of the bar, when he put out to sea.

For though from out our bourne of

Time and Place
The flood may bear me far,
I hope to see my Pilot face to face
When I have crossed the bar.

"The best thing ever written about aging, in my opinion, is Tennyson's marvelous poem 'Ulysses,' in which the old warrior encourages himself and others not to give up on life too soon. He says:

How dull it is to pause, to make an end,
To rust unburnished, not to shine in use!
As though to breathe were life.

A little later he says:

. . . you and I are old;
Old age hath yet his honor and his toil;
Death closes all: but something ere the end,
Some work of noble note may yet
  be done. . . .
Though much is taken, much abides,
  and though
We are not now that strength which in
  old days
Moved earth and heaven, that which we
  are, we are, —
One equal temper of heroic hearts,
Made weak by time and fate, but strong
  in will
To strive, to seek, to find, and not to yield."

Thus ended Dr. Honeywell's talk. Nobody moved for a minute, even to clap. We were too uplifted.

I have dilly-dallied lately about writing a sequel to my book, using the slightest excuse to put off working. But tonight I am inspired — determined not to "rust unburnished," "as though to breathe were life!" It won't be "a work of noble note," but it will be something. I must remember that "though much is taken, much abides." Sometimes it's a little hard to find that which abides, but I will try.

April 2nd

Day before yesterday I had to make a talk about my book in Charleston, and sign copies of the book afterwards. Yesterday I had to make the same talk to a group in Marion, South Carolina, and sign books afterwards, straining to get the inscriptions just exactly right, while making small talk and trying to be attractive.

I came home and fell down on the bed, utterly beat. I found myself remembering a line from an old movie that Sam and I used to laugh over. Two recruits have just finished their first day of drilling at boot camp. They fall onto their cots in exhaustion, and one of the fellows says, "It has, withal, been a busy day." His buddy sighs and says, "It sure, withal, has!"

I went to sleep chuckling.

April 3rd

Most people here are on a first-name basis with each other, but there's one man that all of us call Mr. Weatherby. He doesn't open up. I've been at the same table in the dining room with him a few times, but have found him aloof, very hard to talk to.

I was surprised, therefore, when he came up to me today in the lobby and pressed a note into my hand.

"I liked your book," he said, quietly. "Maybe you can use this in your next." And with that he was gone. The paper said:

> Counselor, to a woman discussing divorce:
> "What are your grounds?"
> "An acre or so."
> "Do you have a grudge?"
> "No, a carport."
> "Does he beat you up?"
> "No, sir! I get up two hours before he does."

Well, what do you know! Mr. Weatherby has a sense of humor. You just never can tell!

April 4th

We have a large porch on the front of our main building, looking out on a park landscaped with typical Low-country trees and shrubs: magnolias, dogwoods, azaleas, and camellias. A few residents

111

Day before yesterday I had to make a talk about my book in Charleston, and sign copies of the book afterwards.

come out to smoke (they can't do it inside); but others seem to enjoy just sitting quietly, digesting their midday meal and resting their eyes on the greenery.

When I got back from the dentist this afternoon, I sat out there to get some fresh air. Sitting near me was a fairly new resident: Imogene Somebody. (I felt lucky to remember even half of her name.) She kept reading a letter over and over, and sniffling. I held out a hand to her, and she squeezed it.

"I'm sorry," she said.

"Don't be," I said. "Crying is the order of the day here. Some days, that is."

"I just had some bad news in this letter."

"Want to talk about it?"

She nodded. "The letter says that my cousin, Betsy Nugent, died last week, up in Virginia. I can hardly believe it. She was the most *alive* person I ever knew. We grew up together — played together — had sleep overs many nights. She was ten months younger, but we were so close. . . . We learned to swim the same day. We taught each other to dance. . . . We were in each other's weddings. . . . She was godmother to my son . . ."

There was a long pause, and she looked at me sadly, "Do you know something, Hattie? I don't believe I want to live in a world that doesn't have Betsy in it!"

She looked so desolate that I hurt for her. What to say?

"Was she sick a long time?"

113

"No! I saw her about three months ago, and she seemed fine. This letter says she had a fast-growing cancer. Why didn't somebody let me know? I don't have any close relatives there anymore, but somebody could have called me. . . . To think," her tears returned, "I, I . . . didn't even . . . get . . . to her, to her funeral!"

She got up and hurried inside, crying softly. I decided there was nothing I could do for her right now. Maybe later. Imogene Who? I must find out her last name and where her room is. I don't think she has gotten to know many people here.

I sighed. Having Imogene go to pieces in front of me, from grief, was just one more thing to keep this from being a good day.

This morning I went to a memorial service in the chapel for Ellen Caine — she of the funny stories, she who could make us laugh no matter how bad we felt. I truly don't know how we're going to make it without her bright spirit to lighten the aging load.

Then, coming out of the chapel, somebody told me that my good friend Tilly had a fall last night and broke her hip. Another "fallen woman." Poor Tilly. I understand it was a very bad break, and she's so frail.

All of this was in addition to my having to skip lunch to go the dentist. I got there on time, waited nearly an hour (in dire dread), and then had the pleasure of hearing and feeling that lovely drill, and learning that I must have a root canal next week.

I wonder how old Robert Browning was when he wrote:

> Grow old along with me!
>   The best is yet to be,
> The last of life, for which the first was
>   made. . . .

Fifty, maybe? When he still had his decent teeth and eyes and ears, his good knees, and a strong bladder? And still had his loved ones and his good friends?

April 5th

I'm ashamed that I let the blues get to me yesterday; but there are days when the dreary end-of-life syndrome seems to rise up and take hold. Usually I can fight it by counting my blessings. This is a wonderful place, and I know I'm lucky to be here with people my own age, who understand me as I understand them, and are supportive. There would be sadness at my age *any*where; and what we have here in the way of nice companionship, spiritual life, kind supervision, and good entertainment couldn't be beat.

I read it somewhere: Pain is inevitable. Misery is optional.

All the same, I hope there will not be too many more days like yesterday.

I checked on Tilly today and was told that she is resting comfortably, but not quite up to having visitors. I mailed her a card.

April 6th

Louly Canfield has been complaining for months about her hearing. Says she's missing too much "good stuff." Finally last week, she broke down and bought a hearing aid. Now she's fussing about the "static," the background noises.

She swears she can hear the pollen falling!

We were talking about the pollen today after a meeting of the library committee. The town of Drayton grew up in a forest of tremendous long-leaf pines. In spite of the loss of hundreds of them in Hurricane Hugo, and the loss of hundreds more to "Progress" (a questionable word in my book), there are plenty of the tall sentinels left for us to enjoy walking under and looking at the moon through. At this time of year, they also contribute to one of our springtime displays — not gorgeous blooms, but a yellow coating of pollen on everything and everybody!

Because of our springtime show of azaleas, camellias, dogwoods, wisteria, and jessamine, Drayton is often called "Flowertown in the Pines." But it would be just as appropriate to call it:

FLOWERTOWN IN THE POLLEN
Those sounds you're hearing, hereabouts,
  Are nothing grave or sinister,
They're issuing from citizens

(Including, yet, our minister!)

The villain is a yellow dust
    That floats upon the breezes.
It irritates both nose and eyes
    And causes snorts and sneezes.

Like all who love the South, I hold
    The pine in veneration,
But wish its sex life didn't include
    So darn much pollination!

Now, *that* (sex life) reminds me of another story that came up in our gathering this afternoon. Some of us were sitting around "yacking," and Christine told us about a fellow in her hometown who was married three times and had a "passel" of children. His oldest daughter told Christine, "Papa had twenty-nine children. He was goin' for thirty, but the mumps went down on him."

We were also talking about other things — in addition to the pollen — that irritate us. It seemed I had opened up a can of worms. We got onto the subject of language, and the eight of us dredged up so many wrong pronunciations and terms, so many boo-boos, that I had to get out my notebook and jot them down. We decided that Americans are entirely too careless in their speech. It's distressing.

Goodness, I suppose such irritability qualifies us for a pretty low C.Q., today anyway.

Overheard: "Now, let me see . . . What was it that I was worrying about a while ago?"

April 8th

We were talking at the table today about what a nice place this home is.

"I'm glad I came when I did," said Ethel. "It nearly killed me to break up my home, but now I know I did the right thing. I feel so safe here."

"I like not having to cook," said Marcia Coleman.

Rose spoke of the caring people on the staff. "They act as if I'm their grandmother."

Somebody mentioned the Assisted Living Hall and the Health Care Center. "They're great, I've *heard*," said Ralph Goodman, "but I don't want to find out any more about them *yet*. I'll have to admit, they do take good care of us here."

"You're right," said Curtis. "When I've been here twenty-five years I'm gonna write 'em a letter of thanks."

Ralph looked at Curtis. "How old are you, man?"

"Eighty-five, come June."

"Well, I'll tell you what, my friend. If I were you, I believe I'd write that letter today, and put it in escrow, or something."

That exchange about Curtis's age reminded me of a cute story.

First Lady: Come on. Break down.
 Tell me how old you are.
Second Lady: Can you keep a secret?
First Lady: Sure!
Second Lady: So can I!

Chapter 8

Much Abides

April 10th

I came upon Ethel in the hall and asked her how she "did."

"Not good. I've got digestive troubles." She put her hand on her stomach. "There's a rumbling and a grumbling."

I went on down the hall, thinking: That sounds like Edgar Allan Poe. "There's a tumbling and a rumbling, as of something faintly grumbling . . ."

April 12th

Mary's door was open. I tapped on it and called out, "Ready to go to lunch?"

"Not quite," she answered. "I want to finish this task." She was bending over a bureau drawer. "I'm rearranging my smalls."

I went on down the hall, thinking about "smalls." I remembered seeing the word in old

English novels. Later, I looked it up in the dictionary. "Small clothes" originally referred to knee britches, but I think, when it turned into "smalls," it came to mean underclothes. Mary's hometown is near the Appalachian Mountains, where so many wonderful old English expressions have hung on. Interesting.

April 13th

It's not a Friday the thirteenth, but there was some bad luck for the golfers today. It involved the disputed putting green, which originally had some residents upset, but was supported by many others and built with Mr. Detwiler's blessing.

I must say, it got used even during the winter by the diehard duffers, and, of course, the lovely spring weather has brought out a host of putters and other putterers. Well, this morning someone *did* break a window in one of the apartments overlooking the courtyard (one of the opponents' dire predictions come true). What a turmoil ensued!

The most cogent account I was able to glean at lunch was that Carl Royster, a nice resident (and well-known sports enthusiast — even at age eighty-plus), had brought his whole bag of golf clubs down. I suppose that should have been a tip-off.

He busied himself with the clubs for a few minutes, and before anyone saw what he was doing, he yelled "Fore" and drove a ball into a window. No one was hurt, *Deo gratias,* but it certainly could have been tragic. Even a ricochet off a wall or a bench could have done some real damage to anyone on the putting green. (Which president was it that hit a spectator with a golf ball? President Ford, I think.)

Anyway, the explosion of glass and the shouting brought Mr. D. out to see what in the world had happened. It was he who realized that Mr. Royster himself needed attention. Dazed, Carl had dropped the golf club and was obviously puzzled by all the commotion. Other staff had come on the scene, and Mr. Detwiler sent one of them to call 911 and bring a doctor from the Health Center.

Mr. Royster is said to be resting comfortably at the hospital, but something is clearly wrong. An event such as this always sends a chill through our population; of course, it could be something as simple as adjusting medication. Let's hope so . . . or at least that he will not linger *non compos mentis.*

Because of the circumstances of what happened, I don't expect the putting-green opponents to garner much sympathy if they choose to go on the attack.

May 5th

It's great fun to open my mailbox these days. I'll never get used to the surprise of getting fan letters! The postmarks are intriguing: Escondido, California; Port Orange, Florida; Cape Girardeau, Missouri; Newfield, Connecticut.

The best ones say things like, "Your little book is priceless," "a gem," "a delight"! I'm not making it up. They *say* that! And I'm more astonished than *any*one!

A number of people in retirement homes have said, "You were writing about us!" Several, slightly younger, have said, "You helped me to make the decision about going to a 'home.' "

One man from Ohio wrote a while back that he liked my book, and then said, "I have written eight novels and haven't been able to get a single one published. Send me the name of your agent."

I wrote him a thank-you note (as I do to all), and said that I didn't even know the name of an agent. He answered immediately, saying, "I've decided to make *you* my agent. You now have your foot in the door. You have an editor. I will send you my latest novel (680 pages), and I want you to send it straight to your editor."

If I'd known his phone number I would have called him up. As it was, I wrote to him by Overnight Mail and said, *Don't send me anything!* I'm a very old lady who can hardly manage her own affairs."

I've heard no more from that address.

It's pleasing that so many people say things like, "Do it again." "Make us laugh some more." A few have even taken the trouble to send me stories, and I'm using some of them in my sequel notes.

The interest and enthusiasm of the folks here at The Home has been another plus. They've kind of adopted the little volume. They noised it all around when the book went into its second printing. They talk as if there's no doubt that it will be made into a movie, with this place as the setting, and they're picking out parts to play! Several have said, "What a pity Jessica Tandy is no longer around, or Helen Hayes." They've even asked me if I think I could play the narrator! I tell them, "Not without two face lifts and a voice transplant."

They're helping me spread the word by sending copies to friends in faraway places.

People are the nicest things!

May 6th

Rose had trouble with the IRS last year, something about taxes on a house that she sold. I think it had to do with something called the Homestead Act, but I'm not sure. Anyway, the Internal Revenue folks sent her a paper stating that they had decided that she did not, after all, owe taxes on that sale.

She held up the legal-looking paper at the lunch table and said, "I've waited so long for this thing, and now that it's here I never want to see it again."

"Tell you what you do, then, Rose," said Curtis, dryly. "Put it in your Bible."

May 10th

We had an argument at the table today about the pronunciation of the word "amen." Rose said she likes "ah-men." I said I think people are putting on when they say "ah-men."

"Why?" she asked.

"Well, they think it sounds better — but it's really not correct. Look it up in the dictionary."

Rose said it was too late for her to change. I persisted that I really think it ought to be cleared up. It's too bad to hear the word said two different ways at the end of a public prayer. So, after lunch, Rose and I stopped by the library to do a little research.

We pulled two dictionaries off the shelf and both got surprised. The one I looked in, much to my chagrin, gave "ä" first, while Rose found preference given to the long "a." The preferences in the dictionaries were different — as are Rose's and mine — but both books did list *both* pronunciations. We agreed to disagree on the issue!

In our further conversation, however, we found that we do agree on our versions of the Lord's Prayer. The Presbyterians ask to be forgiven their "debts," while the Episcopalians come out several syllables behind, saying, "Forgive us our trespasses."

I asked a minister about that once. He said, "Well, the first Presbyterians were Scottish. You know very well that we Scots were and are more concerned with money and debts than we are with mere trespasses."

I won't give the minister's name, but it had a "Mc" in front of it.

May 12th

I came upon Gusta in The Home's post office. "How're you doing?" I asked.

She made a face. "Oh, I'm breathing in and breathing out. That's about all I can manage these days."

Later, I met Marcia coming out of the dining room giggling.

"Tell me," I said. "I need to laugh."

"Well," she said, "Geneva has been asking me for days to drive her to Wal-Mart for something she needed badly. Today I said, 'Neva, my car is fixed now. I can take you shopping. What is it you want to get?' Geneva hung her head and said, 'I can't remember.' And then she raised up her head and glared at me and said, 'If you just hadn't taken so *long* . . .' "

Trust Neva to blame anybody but herself.

May 19th

We had cherry cobbler for dessert today, and that reminded some of us of the chef-before-last, the man who was our chef when I came here. He loved to put on fancy dinners at Valentine's,

Christmas, any old time. He would even do ice sculptures occasionally.

On my first Fourth of July here, he told us we were to have a scrumptious, festive dessert to top off our dinner. We really looked forward to the surprise, which turned out to be Cherries Jubilee. But, alas! Even though he lit match after match, the lovely desserts wouldn't flame up.

It turned out that somebody had gotten into his stock of brandy and watered it, after helping themselves. I'll tell you what: that was one incensed chef. His fancy cherries didn't flame up, but *he* did. They told me that people in the kitchen stepped lightly around him for days.

May 25th

We were sitting around the lunch table today reminiscing about Carl Royster, who died yesterday.

"Carl was lucky in the way he went," said Curtis. "He was a Braves fan, and he was sitting in an easy chair in his hospital room, in front of the TV, watching live baseball — and the Braves were winnin'!"

A good way to go, we agreed.

After the incident with the golf ball last month, doctors discovered a blood clot that was affecting Carl's brain. He was still being treated with blood thinners and other medications, but he was not in pain, nor had he had a further attack. The news was that his heart had just stopped. What a lucky man! No heroic measures to keep him going, maybe injured and miserable.

We began to talk about ways we would like to spend our last minutes on this planet, minutes that we know we face any time now. Still, it wasn't a lugubrious conversation.

"I can tell you what I'd like to be doing in that last minute," said Mary Dunlap. "I'd like to be eating the last spoonful of a grand helping of chocolate mousse!"

We laughed. Mary loves to eat, and she's a choc-o-holic.

Ralph Goodman said, "What I'd like to be doing, in my last minute, is to be at the Clemson-Carolina football game, on my feet, yellin', because Clemson just made another touchdown that made the score Clemson 26, Carolina 0, in the fourth quarter." Ralph is a true Clemson alum.

"What about you, Hattie?" somebody asked.

"Well — I can think of a lot of good last minutes. . . . One of them would be to be listening to a perfect recording of Arthur Rubinstein playing *Traumerei*."

"That would suit me, too," said Cecil, "with my hearing aid in and working."

"I'll tell you what would suit me," said Ethel, wrinkling her nose. She has retained her tip-tilted nose, and her rare smile. "At that moment I'd like to be in the midst of a dream. I'd like to be dreaming that I was eighteen, and I was dancing a fast fox-trot, or maybe a little jitterbug, at the old pavilion on Pawley's Island, with about a zillion stags lined up and waiting to tap my partner on the shoulder! Honey, I just hope Heaven will be that good!"

We had to laugh. We could see the cute young Ethel, a real "flapper," doing the "Charleston," with hair and legs flying.

Curtis shook his head and said, "You-all can conjure up all the last minutes you want to, but I don't want t' think about 'em. I'm not gonna do any packin', either."

We had to laugh.

I looked around at my tablemates, thinking: How lucky I am, to be spending my old age among lighthearted people like these!

Later

One of our gentlemen, having just gotten over an illness, was sitting on the bench outside the dining room, waiting with a number of other residents for the doors to open. He reached down to scratch his leg.

"Oh, my God!" he yelled. "I must be having another stroke! I can't feel a thing!"

"No wonder," said the lady sitting next to him in the tight line. "That's *my* leg you're scratchin'!"

May 27th

Today's steady, soaking rain (the kind that's good for the farmers this time of year), coupled with yesterday's conversation about great "last moments," kept me inside and in a thoughtful mood. I looked through my Bartlett's and other books and came across some wonderful quotations.

George Bernard Shaw said, "I want to be thoroughly used up when I die. . . . Life is no brief candle to me, it is sort of a splendid torch. I want to make it burn as brightly as I can. . . . "

Here's one by Virgil: "Age carries all things, even the mind, away."

I looked up Virgil's statistics. He only lived forty-nine years. To Publius Virgilius, I say: Son, you didn't know the half of it!

And yet . . . Wait just a minute, Mr. Virgil. I've been thinking. Even when age dulls the mind — takes away the sharpness — there is something left that youth does not have. I keep remembering Tennyson's Ulysses saying: "Though much is taken, much abides."

There are memories of things that only we ancients can know, of a time when the world was a sweeter place. When there was more politeness and less crime; more playing fields and less traffic; more modesty and less pornography. In a place like FairAcres, there are a myriad of such memories. Some of them were aired the time we had our Recollections Night. Maybe we should have more such nights. Or, better still, we should write our treasured memories down, and thus refute Virgil's claim.

I remember when there were more things like

hayrides and Sunday School picnics, and cook-outs with neighbors and friends, followed by sing-alongs; when there was more trust and less suspicion. That last phrase reminds me that I can remember my family going to the beach for a month and not even locking our front door when we left home!

Speaking of going to the beach for a month, Retta came this afternoon and had a cup of tea and a visit, and I asked her if Sidney was going to the beach in August with his children and grandchildren. She says he is.

He has continued to squire her around, and they enjoy the occasional morning of golf. I've even seen her sitting in the courtyard visiting while Sidney practices on the putting green. Though Paul is now completely mobile after re-covering from his broken ankle, Retta and Sidney continue regular Meals-on-Wheels deliveries. She said Paul has offered to do the route with her while Sidney is away.

May 31st

Miss Lucy, in the infirmary, is eighty-five — but do you think she will let the doctor come into her room without a nurse? Not on your life.

"Do you think I'm gonna let *him* unbutton my night gown? The very idea!"

Chapter 9

With a Song . . .

June 5th

Some of our "inmates" have been asking Sidney
to invite "that nice Mr. Stringfellow" to come out
again and lead some singing.

Christine Summers — no mean singer herself
— said in one conversation, "I have a feeling he
knows some rare old songs — some out-of-print,
handed-down things we'd love to hear, and his
voice has such a pleasing quality. Do ask him to
come, Sidney. I'll help you arrange it."

So, last night found Ben — washed, shined,
and smiling — sitting on the bench in front of
the baby-grand piano in our lobby, with at least
a hundred elderly people gathered around in fold-
ing chairs. He plucked tentatively, softly, on the
strings of his guitar. I could tell he was a little
apprehensive.

"Where's your ukulele?" someone asked.

"Well, sir, I thought in honor of this occasion

I'd git out my box. Mr. Metcalf helped me git it down from a high shelf. Ev'ry string was busted." (He said that old-timey "hepped" and "strang.")

Ben plucked and listened and tuned. Then he looked up at us and said, "As you can see, he went somewhere and fetched some strings — and here I am, ready or not! I hope y'all are gonna sing with me."

"We will," said Chris, "but first we'd love to hear some songs you brought down with you from the mountains. That would be a treat."

"I don't know about a treat," said Ben, smiling. "More like a trick, the way my throat behaves these days. Anyway, do any of ye remember an old song — a ballid from England, I reck'n — called 'Lord Lovel'?"

There was a general shaking of heads.

"Well, I'll tell you somethin', folks. If it's an example of an old English song, I'm not surprised we beat 'em, back in the Revolution." He strummed a chord, and started:

"Lord Lovel he stood at his castle gate
A-combin' his milk-white steed,
When along came Lady Nancy-Belle,
For to bid her lover good speed,
    speed, speed,
For to bid her lover good speed.

'Oh, where are you going, Lord Lovel?' she cried,
    'Oh, where are you going?' cried she.

133

Ben plucked and listened and tuned.

'I'm going a-travelling, Nancy-Belle,
Strange countries for to see, see, see,
Strange countries for to see.' "

Ben paused and said, "Well, folks, I'm not a-gonna sing about all the strange countries he went for to see, on that milk-white steed; but he finally came home, and the last of it goes like this:

Lady Nancy-Belle she died today,
Lord Lovel he died tomorrow.
Lady Nancy-Belle she died of grief,
Lord Lovel he died of sorrow, of sorrow.
Lord Lovel he died of sorrow.

They put him in the cold church yard,
They buried her in the byre,
And out of her breast there grew a red rose,
And out of his grew a briar, briar, briar,
And out of his grew a briar.

They grew and grew to the church-steeple
  top
And when they could grow no higher,
There they entwined in a true lovers' knot
For all good folks to admire, -mire, -mire,
For all good folks to admire."

As the final chord died, there was a round of clapping, which Ben acknowledged shyly.
"So," he said, "that's the story of Lord Lovel.

I thought it was kinda sad that the gentleman could only produce a briar!" Appreciative laughs ran through the crowd.

"Let's see. If ye like oldies, here's a right nice one."

He sang sweetly, "Charlie's My Darlin', the Young Chevalier." The people showed him that they liked it.

"Here's another'n I think came from England." It was "Greensleeves," and the way Ben sang it was plaintive and touching. It brought much applause and a few scattered voices joining in on some lines.

"My mama used to sing one that went like this.

Oh, don't you remember Sweet Alice,
  Ben Bolt?
Sweet Alice, whose hair was so brown?
Who wept with delight when you gave her
  a smile,
And trembled with fear at your frown?"

He looked up and smiled. "I'll tell you somethin', folks. Even as a little tyke I wondered what kind of a creature Sweet Alice was — cryin' when you smiled at her, and tremblin' if you so much as frowned! She was a big ninny, if you ask me! I never cared much for Sweet Alice."

He strummed and tuned for a minute.

"One that I do care for was written by Mr. Robbie Burns. Now that was a fellow with a heart! Come on, folks, sing 'Flow Gently' with me."

And some of them did, softly bidding the Sweet Afton to disturb not Mary's dream.

That was followed by "Just a Song at Twilight." Everybody seemed to know that beloved one.

A voice called out, "How about some Stephen Foster?"

"Yes, *ma'am*," said Ben, and launched into "Way down upon the Swanee River. . . ." That was followed by "My Old Kentucky Home." I saw some tears on a good many cheeks.

"Now let's get a little harmony goin'," said Ben. "I need somebody to 'alto in behind the bass.' And a tenor. Is there a tenor in the crowd?" Two men held up their hands. "OK! I reck'n y'all know 'Annie Laurie'? If you don't remember the words, just hum along."

Well, sir, it was beautiful! Most people were able to sing the first verse. Then Ben lined out the words of the second verse:

". . . And dark blue was her e'e,
And for bonny Annie Laurie
I'd lay me doon and dee."

In spite of quavery voices, it was lovely. And I saw Sidney reach over and gently take Retta's hand. She didn't withdraw it.

Ben brushed tears from his own eyes, played some fast chords, and said, "Come on, ev'rybody. Let's snap it up a little. Here's a foot stomper, 'Buffalo Gals, Won't You Come Out Tonight?' "

We sang along with him, clapping and tapping our feet. Then he struck up, "Good Night, Ladies."

"Oh, no!" somebody said. "It's too early!"

"No, sir," said Ben. "Bull-bat time's long gone, and my throat has give out. But I've enjoyed bein' here. We dug up some old'uns, didn't we? And some good'uns, too."

There was a chorus of agreement and much applause. He was asked if he would come back, and he promised he would. Most stayed for refreshments and visiting afterward. But Retta excused herself. I "swan," as my grandmother used to say, I can't figure my old friend out.

We had thoroughly enjoyed the "sangin'." Ben remembered so many old-time tunes, songs we had heard our parents and grandparents sing, songs some of us had learned in glee clubs. I kept thinking of ones I'd like us to try when he comes again, songs like "Down in the Diving Bell" and "Aura Lee" and "Come Where My Love Lies Dreaming."

August 5th

I haven't had much time to write in this journal lately. A first novel by an eighty-five-year-old lady must be "novel." I'm getting requests for all kinds of appearances, plus book-signings. Some I've had to turn down, for lack of time and strength.

I'm overwhelmed by the attention the little book is getting in newspapers and magazines, coast-to-coast, even though I have no agent to push it. People have sent me copies of thirty-nine feature articles and rave reviews that have appeared in all the big papers except my home-area "rag," the staid *Charleston Post and Courier.* Maybe they will eventually break down.

The *Atlanta Journal-Constitution* ran a good book review, and then sent a reporter and photographer to spend a half-day with me, for a feature article — three columns! The photographer said she wanted a shot of me sitting at my typewriter. I groaned.

"You can't go in that little room," I said. "Something is liable to bite you!"

She insisted. I said, "That tiny utility room is my office, my laundry (complete with washer and dryer), my storage room, and my junk room. It's Litter City. *Please,* not in there!" But she still insisted, and of course the picture the paper used was the one taken in the litter.

The most exciting event was being invited to Chicago to read excerpts and sign books at the American Booksellers Association convention. People were so nice to me — especially the ones from the publishing house in Atlanta. I had never been to Chicago before. In June, it was cool, with low humidity — a break from our steaming Low-country. I will never forget the view of the stunning city from a boat on Lake Michigan.

Except for my being a little addled by the crowds at the convention (all the bookstore owners in the U.S. were there, I'm sure — and their spouses and chief clerks), it was a great two days. Too short. I didn't even get to Marshall Field's!

Because the third printing is going "great guns," the publisher has asked me for a sequel. I'm now gathering notes in earnest, and am asking all my friends for stories. I hope people won't start groaning or clamming up when they see me coming.

One great result of the publication is the stream of letters I'm still getting from all over the country. I simply can't believe it! And of course, if people are nice enough to let me know they like my book, I have to sit right down and answer every single note, which consumes time I should be spending on the new project.

Some of the people I hear from live in retirement homes like this one. Several have said, "You were writing about *us*. We read it aloud and whooped. Shed a tear or two, also." These responses are very gratifying. If I wake up and find that it has all been a dream — which well could be — then at least it has been one heck of a reverie!

August 7th

There's a man in the infirmary, Larry Stover, age ninety, who says he still likes to see pretty girls come in the door, even if he can't remember why! Recently he was told that his heart was bad and that he needed a pacemaker. He was offered one that would last about ten years, or a more expensive one that might last twenty years. He went for the twenty-year one. Talk about optimism! Maybe he's hoping that the costly appliance will cause him to remember why he likes to see pretty girls.

August 10th

Today was the first opportunity I have had lately to have a long talk with Retta. I have heard things this summer about "the romance," but have made a real effort not to listen to speculation. I knew that when we had time together — and she felt so disposed — Retta would fill me in.

She and I went out on the terrace this evening, after our early supper. We sat and admired the urns filled with rosy geraniums that have withstood the heat, with much watering and care.

Sidney had left last week to spend a month at Nag's Head with his family.

"Do you miss him?" I asked.

"You know I do! He's a very 'missable' person. . . . But Hattie, I'm trying hard not to think about him."

"Why?"

"Because I don't want to become dependent on him. I'm convinced it would be best for us to be good friends, and nothing more."

"But you miss him?"

"I told you I did."

"How much?" I persisted.

Before she could answer, we noticed a pearl-gray Chrysler New Yorker pulling into the parking lot in front of The Home.

"Isn't that Sidney's car?" I asked.

"It couldn't be!"

But it *was* Sidney Metcalf, looking a little tired and windblown, coming toward us, smiling. Us? He didn't even know I was there. He made for Retta, his eyes devouring her.

"But you were supposed —"

"I know. I was due to stay three more weeks, but I'll tell you something, my dear. What with mosquitoes and sunburn and rambunctious teenagers, I did well to last seven days. And I think they were glad to get rid of fussy old Grandpa."

I went inside after making an excuse, which they didn't even hear. I'm sure it was not the sun and insects and noise that brought Sidney back. What ails him was caused by the bite of a love-bug — one of the most ferocious bites I have ever encountered. And at our age!

September 6th

I saw Paul and Curtis heading for the terrace after supper tonight, so I headed for my perch in the library, near the open window, where I could eavesdrop.

"How are you doing?" asked Paul.

"Not so good." Curtis sighed. "I reckon I'm 'nearer my God to thee.' "

"Oh, no, man! You're not that far gone! What's the matter?"

"Trouble with my prostrate."

I'm sure Paul knew that Curtis meant "prostate," but he didn't correct him. I began to squirm a little. For the first time I felt guilty about listening.

"I'm sorry to hear that," said Paul. "I was reading in *Time* yesterday about a new treatment for that malady. Maybe you can be helped. How long have you had trouble?"

"About ten months, I reckon."

"And you haven't even mentioned it to me."

"Well — I hear people around here advertisin' their troubles — givin' 'organ recitals' — and I just figured, since they couldn't help me anyway, I'd just stay quiet."

"Hmmmm . . ." said Paul. After a couple of minutes, he said, "You know something, Curtis? Hattie McNair is getting up questions for some kind of Contrariness test. Maybe you and I could write one for her like this: 'Can you keep quiet about something that might interest the busybodies, but that really concerns only you and your doctor?' "

"Yeah. I bet Hattie could use that."

I nodded my head vigorously as I sat in my chair inside. I could use it.

"Man!" said Curtis. "Look at the end of that sunset! That coloration is a sight! Look how it's makin' those clouds glow! . . . My mother used to say 'Pretty enough to draw and paint!' "

143

They were quiet for a while, and then Paul said, "I see you're not smoking tonight. How come? Haven't you been smoking most of your life?"

"Sixty years, I reckon," said Curtis. "I just decided yesterday that it might get to be a bad habit, so I quit."

On that good line I left them and came upstairs to do some "jotting."

September 14th

We have changed the name of the Sew-Around Circle to The G.O.G.'s — The Good Old Girls — and we have invited Retta to join us. (She does a mean cross-stitch.)

Of course, people are always consumed with interest about her courtship with Sidney, or, rather, his pursuit of her. I always keep quiet and respect her privacy and her confidences, but today, as we busied our hands with various projects, some bold person said, "Come on, Retta. Be big-hearted. Tell us what you and Sidney did yesterday after your Meals-on-Wheels deliveries."

She hesitated a minute, and then smiled. "Well, I suppose it's worth telling. We went across the Cooper River to Mount Pleasant and had dinner in a restaurant that overlooks Shem Creek and the shrimp boats. We sat at a large window and watched the sunset. Then coming home it was dark, and the two up-and-down bridges were lit up and looked like sparkling

144

necklaces. It was really lovely."

There were sighs and smiles around the circle. I suppose it is better to sniff romance in the air than just to smell liniment or cough syrup or the stuff they grease wheelchair wheels with.

One person near me, who shall remain nameless, whispered, "Some people have all the luck." Her tone of voice troubled me. Another question for the C.Q. test could be: "Are you willing to count your own blessings and not be too envious of another's good fortune?"

September 15th

We have a good security service here, nice guards who watch out for us and who ride bikes around the grounds of the place, circling about once an hour, day and night, to make sure all is well.

One of the guards, Billy Stuart, wears khaki shorts all summer. Today was rather cool, and when he appeared in khaki pants, one of our "malaprop-ing" ladies called out to him, in all innocence, "Oh, Billy! I hardly know you with your pants on!"

September 17th

Many mornings I get up, bathe, get dressed, go to breakfast or fix my own, read the paper — and then I want to go back to bed! Nine-thirty in the A.M., and I'm looking at those sheets and that downy pillow longingly. Isn't that awful? Some mornings I crawl back in for a half-hour snooze that is not very sweet because my conscience is hovering.

I try to tell myself, paraphrasing Mr. Longfellow: Life is real, life is earnest, and the *bed* is not its goal! But the bed is so tempting to old bones. Oh, me. I'll never get a sequel finished at this rate.

I also have another temptation: any good book. When I ought to be writing, I'm reading. I suppose, like eating candy, reading is a habit that started too early to be broken now.

September 22nd

Our conversation today turned into a contest: Whose memory was the best? Who could recall back the furthest?

We talked about comics — only we called them "funny papers."

"I can even remember 'Mutt and Jeff,' " said Ethel.

"I go back further than that," said Christine, "all the way to 'Maggie and Jiggs'!"

"That's nothing!" said Paul. "I even remember 'The Katzenjammer Kids'! What were their names?"

"Hans and Fritz!" I called out triumphantly. "There was a little, short, fat fellow — was he called The Professor?"

It didn't take long to proceed from funnies to

old movies, always a favorite category for reminiscing.

"I'll bet I can name a woman who played in early movies with Charlie Chaplin and Buster Keaton," I announced proudly, "— not the heroine, the ugly woman, tall and gangly. Anybody remember? No? Her name was Flora Finch!"

"Boy, are we dating ourselves!" said Ethel. After a minute, with a faraway look, she said, "I remember Mama taking me to see *The Birth of a Nation* when I was six years old. I remember how she cried. She taught me that it was a sin not to clap when 'Dixie' was played, and a sin to sing 'Marching Through Georgia!' "

"Wasn't it funny," said Tilly (she is using a walker now, but she gets about well) "the way there was always somebody in the movie audience who would read the captions out loud? Laboring over any word longer than two syllables?"

We talked about *Our Gang*, and about Fatty Arbuckle, and about Pearl White in *The Perils of Pauline.*

"Isn't it *some*thing?" Christine said. "We can dig up those names from seventy-five years ago, and I can't remember the name of the new woman in the apartment next to mine! I've met her three times, and if she came along right now I couldn't introduce you to her."

I know what you mean," said Tilly. "I can't even remember my social security number, or what day to put my laundry bag in the hall."

"Right," agreed Christine, sadly. "Do you know — I'm ashamed to admit it, but sometimes I can't even remember my darling granddaughter's name! I was trying to introduce two people last week, and I was horrified to hear myself saying, 'I want you to meet my dear friend What's-Her-Name.' "

Later

Now that I'm back in my quarters, I'm thinking about the compartments of our memories: the long-ago so clear, the near-time so fleeting. . . . Forgive me, God, but I think there could be a better arrangement.

I'm also thinking about that cute little Energizer rabbit in the TV ad. Like him, we go on and on, but part of our apparatus is running down, and there seems to be no way to recharge it.

Sometimes I get put out with myself for not being able to remember something; and many times I get impatient with someone else for the same reason. Why is she taking so long to answer me? Or: Why can't he think of it *today?* He just told us about it at the table yesterday!

Maybe a question for the Contrariness Quotient test could be: "Can you be patient with people whose memories are slipping, just as yours is?"

We've all been worried about Rose, who has been ill with a very serious case of pneumonia. She was in the hospital, then the Health Care Center, and is now, finally, back in her room.

When I went to see her after church today, I intended to stay only a minute. She looked so small and frail, in her French blue embroidered bathrobe, sitting at her desk — a cherry-wood secretary that I have always coveted.

"I don't want to tire you," I said.

"I'm really glad to see you, Hattie," she declared. "I had reached an impasse here, in what I was trying to do. Maybe a little break will help." She turned her chair around to face me. "Don't tell me. I know. I should've cleared these drawers out years ago, before I moved here. I couldn't quite face it, so I told the movers just to tape the drawers shut. . . . This desk has been mine for forty-nine years, since I inherited it from my grandmother. It's way too big for this room. I know that; but I couldn't bring myself to part with it.

"These lower drawers hold my whole life! And look here . . ." She turned and fiddled with one of the fancy little cubbyholes and the board in back of it. "Voilà! A secret drawer!"

I was fascinated, but I could tell she was tiring. She seemed to think she must hurry now, after putting off this clearing-out job too long.

I had brought a bottle of Harvey's Bristol

Cream sherry, and persuaded her to let me open it and pour us each a glass. In a little while, I helped her back to bed and promised to come again tomorrow.

October 2nd

When I went to Rose's room today she was back at her desk. One of the lower drawers was half open, and she was pulling things out of it.

"This is killing me, Hattie! Look at this." She handed me a faded second-grade report card. "Look!" she said, tears streaming. She pointed to handwritten words on the back: "A lovely little pupil," the teacher had written.

"That was my Cynthia," Rose said.

I knew that Cynthia had died of breast cancer, two years ago.

This won't do, I thought. I took the report card and put it to one side.

"Aren't there any happy memories in that scrap drawer?" I asked.

She sighed and ran her hands through the collection of aging papers, letters, and photographs.

"Here's a card from Edward, from summer camp. I think he was nine — maybe ten." She wiped her eyes with a handkerchief and began to smile as she read.

"It says, 'Please send me some mony. Send me a better piller, this one is hard. I will go kinooing today.' He was only going to be there another week, and he wanted me to mail him a pillow!"

We both smiled, and she dropped the card into the wastebasket, reluctantly.

The next thing she dug out was a dainty folded card: a dance card, with a tiny pencil attached by a now-pale blue satin ribbon. "There's no date," she said, examining the card. "It must have been one of the Harvest Balls." She ran her fingers lovingly over the names scrawled on the lines and shook her head. Her mouth trembled. "These boys. These darling boys. Hattie — they're all gone! Not a one left to dance with me . . . ever again —"

I couldn't help thinking that they wouldn't be able to do much dancing with her if they were living. She'd probably have to hold them up; but I knew how she felt. There's nothing more nostalgic than a faded dance card. I had thrown away a few myself in recent years.

When I came back to my apartment, after helping Rose all I could, I pulled out from under my bed the Campbell Soup box containing the entire memorabilia of my life. I fingered various items, and picked up a page that had been torn from a magazine. It was from *The Youth's Companion*, dated July 1924, and on it were several short poems. One was by Harriet Allston. That was me!

I shook my head over the childish lines. Anyway, my folks had been pleased at my "publication." I threw the paper away.

Next I picked up a fancy ruffled ribbon — a once-white, now-yellowed bow that had graced a long-dead corsage. . . . Oh, dear. Why had I kept *that* one, to stab me with the heartbreak of that ancient evening?

I marched over to the wastebasket and dropped it in. I ended up throwing away half of the contents of that box.

I wondered if my children would have even this many memories saved. They don't do much saving of "stuff" these days. No attics to put it in. Maybe they're better off. They won't have the kind of heartbreaking time that Rose is experiencing now.

From one of the snatches-of-poetry recesses of my peculiar mind came the lines:

> "Ah, and how we fondly cherish
> Faded things that had better perish."

We should do more perishing, I guess; but as I walked to the dining room a few minutes later, the words of an old song — a tearjerker — came to mind: "Some letters tied with blue, a photograph or two, I find a rose from you, among my souvenirs. . . ."

Oh, dear. You can throw away things, but you can't keep your mind from looking back, sometimes in joy, more times in heart-wrenching sentiment.

Chapter 10

A Caring People

October 8th

There is a delightful private library in Drayton called The Timrod. It was named (nearly a hundred years ago) for Henry Timrod, a Southern poet who lived here for a while.

Every year there is a fundraiser: a book sale and luncheon at the library. Several of us from The Home usually go to it.

Yesterday Gusta Barton, who could be president of a large class of mixer-uppers at this place, was walking through our lobby obviously headed somewhere. Somebody asked her, "Where are you going, so dressed up?"

"I'm going to a luncheon at The Hemroid Library," she announced proudly.

I'm afraid The Timrod will be "The Hemroid" to me from now on.

I believe I get more catalogs than anybody! Especially in the fall leading up to Christmas. Some days there are so many they won't fit into my box, and I get a little note asking me to pick up some mail at the office. It's always so aggravating to wait in line and get only catalogs I don't really want. I used to order some clothes by mail, and the people at those businesses can't seem to forget that. They remain ever hopeful.

Seeing the young, svelte, beautiful models on the cover of one today, I came up with a rhyme.

ORDERING
I see a dress in a catalog.
   It has a certain air —
A dash, a style, a careless grace —
   Jaunty and debonair.

I order it. At last it comes.
   I try it on with glee —
   'I That girl in the catalog
   'auntier than me!

   'ger, and straighter and thinner,
   for any nitpickers in the audi-
   'natical and said ". . . than
   'ed.)

I like the people I'm sitting at table with this go-around. They are interested in politics and current events. One of them actually subscribes to the *Wall Street Journal*. He brings us up to date on a lot of things.

Tonight we had such a serious talk that we stayed on long after we'd finished our dessert and coffee. In fact, the help was standing around glaring at us. We finally told them they could clear everything off and go home — that we'd turn out the lights, but that we had to get this thing settled.

"This thing" was our country's monstrous debt, and we didn't get it settled (of course). We just moaned about the size of it, and the fact that it was growing, even as we spoke.

"I hear," said Paul, "that in seven years there will be no more money for Medicare. I may not be here then. Probably won't be; but I have five grandchildren, and I hate to think of what life may be like for them."

"I know what you mean," said Edwin. "I'm afraid we're a pretty spoiled generation of old people — many of us with a cushy lifestyle that our grandchildren may have to pay for."

"Oh, dear!" said Ethel. "You-all are making me feel terrible. My little great-grandson, Randy, is three. He's adorable. You mean he may have a life of *poverty?*"

"Maybe not real poverty — but he'll be deprived. No doubt about it," said Edwin, shaking his head. "The country can't go on forever existing on borrowed money."

"And here we go, merrily on," I said, "living it up, paying a million dollars or more in interest every day. . . . I understand the president and the Congress are at last working overtime to do something about bringing down the budget. But do you know what I think? I think there won't be a substantial reduction in the national debt until the country's lifestyle is lowered."

There were some lifted eyebrows at that.

"I mean it," I said. "I think all Americans are going to have to pull in their horns and do without, a little bit."

"Old people, too?" asked Ethel.

"Of course," I said. "I agree with Edwin. I get a little tired of seeing elderly people — very healthy-looking people — sounding off in Washington on TV, daring the government to cut a penny from our Social Security payments or our pensions. They seem to feel that a little gray hair gives them immense privilege."

"The trouble is," said Paul, frowning, "there are too many of us. We're living too long."

We looked at each other with troubled faces, knowing that he was probably right.

"Well, they can't just knock us off," said Edwin, "or put us out on the ice on rafts, like I hear the Eskimos used to do."

"Anyway," I said, "I think we oldsters will have to lower our lifestyles along with everybody else. It's going to take sacrifice from *every*body . . .

Don't you remember in the Great Depression, how we had to learn to do without?"

We talked a while about ways people had found to "make do" during those hard days. I said I remembered Mama taking the worn collars off my Dad's shirts and turning them inside-out, so they'd last another few months.

"And sheets!" said Ethel. "A sheet was never thrown away if it began to wear in the middle. My mother tore it apart and sewed the outer edges together. . . . We wore hand-me-down clothes," she added, "and as for food, we ate grits — only we called it hominy — twice a day, with a tiny bit of meat or some kind of hash to help it down."

"I remember that," said Paul. "A chicken was three meals for a good-sized family. Some meat, then hash, then soup with a lot of rice in it."

"And we didn't get so fat!" said Emily, who had been quiet, so far. "Just look at that." She pointed to her middle. "Talk about inflation!"

"We retreaded our tires and made do with the old car for another eight years or so," said Paul. "Sons and fathers had to learn to change oil and work on engines."

We agreed that times were hard then (even disastrous for many people), but it gave us a better sense of values. However, another Great Depression was just what we would like to avoid inflicting on our descendants by some sensible restraint now.

"I'll tell you one big cause of the trouble," said

Edwin, pulling something out of his wallet. He held up a small plastic charge card. "If these things were outlawed, maybe people would get back to living within their means."

"And another thing. I think doctors are going to have to lower their charges a little, to save Medicare. Lord knows they'll still make aplenty."

I mused out loud, "I remember the way everybody pitched in to help in World War II. *Everybody*. It made you proud to be an American. I wonder if our memories — our experiences, and the way we feel — are worth anything? Suppose I write and ask our congressman that? Maybe it's going to take a grassroots movement — a 'What can we do to help?' movement from concerned citizens."

"You write that letter, Hattie. I know you'll say it right," suggested Paul.

"I'll be glad to co-sign it," said Emily.

I questioned the others with my eyes. They all nodded. So, I have a serious job of composing to do, Dear Diary. I'd better get to it.

October 18th

One reason I enjoy eavesdropping on Curtis and Paul, and their after-supper story-swapping, is their colorful choice of words — words they might not use if they knew a lady was listening. (Sometimes I worry a little about that word "lady." Maybe it ought to be "woman with a questionable sense of humor." I used to be a lady;

158

but I lived for forty-four years with a man whose priceless humor was more earthy than genteel. Maybe I lost some gentility, but oh, what I gained in fun!)

Tonight they were talking about a new resident. "She's a nice-enough looking lady," said Paul, "but there's something odd about the way she's built."

"I know what you mean," said Curtis. "She's what an uncle of mine used to call shingle-butted."

Now I know the right name for someone who has no shape in the back — someone who is perfectly straight, all the way down: shingle-butted. Isn't that wonderful? My Sam would have loved it.

Paul said, "When I see a woman shaped like that I always think of Dorena. She was our cook when I was growing up. Completely flat in the back, but, man, how she could cook! I have never tasted anything quite as good as her pineapple fritters and her bread pudding. I loved that woman. . . . I guess what I remember best about Dorena is her baptism. The story of it went all over town.

"Her preacher," Paul continued, "held a revival one Sunday afternoon, and then called for a wholesale baptizing down at the river. The preacher dunked the repentant supplicants in the water, one after the other, but when it came her turn Dorena resisted him. She kept looking down at the water and yelling, 'No, no, sir!'

159

" 'Yield, Sister, yield!' shouted the preacher.

" 'Yeel, nothin'!' said Dorena. 'That ain't no yeel, Preacher! That's a water moccasin!' "

Curtis had a good laugh, slapping his knee and repeating, " 'That ain't no yeel, Preacher.' "

After a minute Paul said, "I remember another story about Dorena. Want to hear it?"

"You know I do."

"One day my brother and I came home from crabbing at the beach, with a tub full of live crabs for Mama and Dorena to cook for supper. Mama put a big pot of water on the stove to heat. Then she and Dorena picked up each crab — claws waving — and dropped it into the boiling water.

" 'This seems so cruel,' said Mama.

" 'They don't mind,' said Dorena. 'They's used to it!' "

November 1st

Well, it wasn't Halloween goblins making us shiver yesterday. It has really turned cold. I got out my heavy coat to go and see Cora in the hospital today.

She has eye trouble, a detached retina. That's certainly not anything to joke about, but we did have a couple of good laughs. Cora said the second day she was there, she heard her roommate talking on the phone. "There's a nice lady in the other bed," the roommate said. "She has a detached rectum."

Cora said she laughed so hard she almost detached her other retina.

I, in turn, told her a story I heard this week at The Home. A new resident told me that she looked at two other places before deciding on FairAcres. She said that at one of the places, the resident who was giving her the tour was lavish in her praise of the facility.

"They do everything for us here," she said. "They watch our health, and if we get a sudden heart attack they even give us artificial insemination!"

November 4th

I'm getting spoiled. If I don't find three or four fan letters in my mailbox every day, I'm real disappointed! Today these were the postmarks: Edmond, Oklahoma; Bradford, Pennsylvania; and DeLand, Florida. All said that they liked my little book and asked me to, "Write another. Make us laugh again." I'm trying. I'm trying.

But maybe I'd better remember something Ann Landers said: "You should treat flattery like chewing gum. Enjoy it, but don't swallow it."

Later

I wasn't at the table where this happened, but I heard about it. Our grapevine here is *strong*. It seems that as they ate, some people in the group were discussing the Romance.

Someone said, "If Retta and Sidney *do* get married, I wonder where they will live? In her apartment or his apartment?"

Somebody else said, "Maybe they will be lucky enough to get one of the cottages on the back campus."

Dr. Browning raised his eyes from his ice cream and said, "Well, just so long as it's near a good school."

He said it so seriously and solemnly that it was a full minute before the table burst into laughter.

November 9th

Ben Stringfellow won't be coming back to us for a while because of a tragic fire. When Sidney and Retta went to the Episcopal Church yesterday to pick up the meals to deliver, they were told not to take a meal to Mr. Stringfellow. There had been a fire, and he was in the hospital.

Retta told me that when they'd finished their route, they hurried to the county hospital where they found Ben in bed, with his hands bandaged, being administered oxygen. He could barely talk, but he managed to let them know that Jeffrey and Jamie's grandmother had gone to sleep sitting too close to a portable heater. The afghan over her legs had apparently touched the heater, then ignited the chair, the rug, the whole place.

By the time Ben smelled the smoke the house was ablaze. He managed to get the children out, but he was afraid they were badly injured.

"They're somewhere in this hospital," he said,

in jerks, clearly very upset. "Will you . . . see . . . what you can . . . find out?"

"Of course," said Sidney. "What about the grandmother?"

"Gone," said Ben. "I went back . . . and tried. Too late. I'm afraid . . . about the boys . . ."

"You take it easy," said Sidney. "We'll be right back."

Retta said her heart was in her throat. They raced to the children's ward and were told that the little boys had serious burns: Jeffrey's on his chest, and Jamie's on his back, but that they were both stable and doing all right.

Jeffrey's eyes lit up when he saw his visitors, but Retta said he was a pitiful sight, bandaged and scared. He pointed to Jamie in the next bed. "Jamie has to lie on his stummick. He burnt his back. If it hadn't been for Mister Ben . . ."

Sidney and Retta stayed a while, comforting the boys as best they could. Jamie had to twist his neck to see them, and he was whimpering; but they were able to report to Ben that the little patients were getting the best of care and that they would recover.

Slowly and painfully, Ben asked, "Was . . . their mother . . . with them? She was out . . . gallivantin' . . . last night."

"No," answered Sidney. "The nurse said she had been there but had left to see about getting her mother buried."

"Oh, Hattie," Retta concluded her sad story, "isn't it tragic? Two beautiful children being left with an alcoholic!"

"She was punished," I said. "I'm sure that's a terrible way to die."

November 13th

Our people at The Home were distressed to hear about Ben.

"That nice man. What a shame!" Christine said when I saw her in the post office. "How badly is he hurt, Hattie?"

"He has some burns on his hands — not too bad. I believe the worst damage was to his lungs. He has lung trouble anyway, and he inhaled a lot of smoke. He's on oxygen, and can hardly talk. Of course, he's terribly worried about the little Davis boys. Ben has some kind of insurance, but the boys don't. Their mother is a waitress, and her job carries no health coverage."

The sad news about the little burned boys began to circulate through The Home. We're a caring people, and it wasn't long before a movement was started to help them *and* their nice self-appointed guardian. Several of us met in the library this afternoon.

"We could take up a collection," said Christine, "but I believe Mr. Stringfellow would be pleased if he heard we had some fun doing it! How about another Recollections evening?"

Paul suggested including some stories as well as actual recollections.

That idea met with everyone's approval, and

December 1st has been set for Storytelling Night. That should fall between any Thanksgiving trips and Christmas travels. And it will give people time to find some tales worth relating or reading. Our Recollections Night last year was such a success — both in monetary results to help Arthur and Dollie Priest, and in enjoyment — that everyone is enthusiastic about a repeat.

"There'll be more leeway this time," said Chris. "Last time we were limited to actual memories, but not now. Anything goes. Any story worth repeating: actual or fictional, written or remembered."

"Pure or profane?" asked Paul.

"Let your conscience be your guide!" said Chris.

November 15th

Sidney and Retta have been busy. They located Evalina Davis, the little boys' mother, at the funeral home. Retta told me that she was pathetic. "I admit I was angry when we approached her," Retta said, "but I couldn't help feeling sorry for her. Hattie, she's only twenty-three years old!

"When Sidney and I told her that we would pay for her mother's funeral, she went to pieces. She said, 'I didn't know what I was going to do. I didn't know where to turn.'

"I asked her if there was any other relative who might help her with the children, and she shook her head again. 'I've got a cousin that works in a knitting mill up near Spartanburg. She's been tryin' to get me to come up there. Said she could get me a job on the machines — but she said she couldn't help me with the boys. I've been wantin' to go, but I didn't know what to do with my kids. Looks like I can't take care of them and myself, too, now that Mama's gone. I'm stayin' with a girlfriend in one room. I don't know what's gonna happen.' Then she started crying.

" 'Would you be willing to put the boys up for adoption?' Sidney asked her.

" 'I been thinkin' about that — anyway, about foster care. Maybe that'd be the best thing right now, till I get a little better off.' "

November 21st

I'm quite touched at the depth of affection that two elderly people have developed for two little almost-abandoned children. I understand it better after going with them to the hospital today, and seeing the way four bright eyes lit up at the sight of people who care for them. They have had little enough of real caring in their lives.

Jamie can now lie on his back, and he was almost buried under stuffed animals that Retta had brought the day before. They kept asking about "Mister Ben." Sidney said, "He's doing all right. He's worried about you two. They're going to bring him by here in a wheelchair today to see you fellows before he leaves."

"Leaves?" Jeffrey asked, apprehensive.

*Jamie can now lie on his back, and he was almost
buried under stuffed animals that Retta had
brought the day before.*

"They're moving him to the Veterans' Hospital in Charleston. That doesn't mean he's any worse. He's a veteran — he fought in the war — so that's where he belongs," explained Sidney. "But he wouldn't leave without checking on you boys."

They looked large-eyed and troubled. "Where's our Mama?" Jamie asked.

"She'll be coming back to see you," said Retta. "But right now, look at this!" She opened a large bag of blown-up balloons and tied them to the beds. "And look at this!" She opened another bag filled with storybooks, brightly illustrated. "I'm coming tomorrow, and I'll read you every single story."

I glanced at Sidney. He was looking at Retta with his heart in his eyes. She looked so pretty in her Castleberry suit, the same violet as her eyes. As usual, she was utterly unconscious of her loveliness.

Chapter 11

High Hopes

November 22nd

What an amazing day this has been! This morning Arthur Priest called me from the maintenance department and asked if he could see me. I told him to give me twenty minutes and come on up.

He arrived and wouldn't accept any coffee. I could tell he had something on his mind.

"Miz McNair, you and the others here have been so good to our family . . . Miss Canfield teaching me to read . . . you all findin' that house and makin' it possible for us to live there —"

"Well, Arthur," I reminded him, "you have been helpful and kind to many of *us,* don't forget. That's why folks at The Home responded in the first place."

"I appreciate that, Miz McNair, I do. And I love workin' here with all of you."

At that point, my heart sank. I just knew that Arthur had found another, better paying position somewhere. He is such a treasure. Not only can he fix *anything,* but he is always happy to help and makes you feel that your request is no trouble at all. Goodness! What would we do without him!

"Dollie and I have been discussin' something," he continued, "and we agreed that you were the person for us to talk to and see what you think about our idea. Then, if you don't mind, maybe you could talk to the others for us."

Oh, dear! I thought. This sounds serious.

"Well, we don't know if what we'd like to do is possible, legally and all, but Dollie and I want to help those little boys — Jeff and Jamie. We'd like to have them come and stay with us — for as long as they need some place."

"Oh, Arthur!" I beamed. "You may just be the answer to some prayers. Are you sure you and your family want to make such a generous offer?"

"Yes, ma'am," he smiled back at me. "Dollie and I have even talked to our boys about it, and they are real excited about the idea. Our house isn't huge, but we have room, and I've been thinking I could fix up a fine place in the attic for all the boys."

"I know Mr. Metcalf has talked to the boys' mother about their future, Arthur, and I don't know what her plans are . . . or how she would feel about any of this. Let me talk to Sidney and to Mrs. Gooding and find out what I can."

"Thank you so much, Miz McNair. We knew you'd be the person to come to."

I told Arthur that I would get right to work and would call him later today. When he left, I felt so exhilarated I had to sit and calm myself for a few minutes. To tell you the truth, Dear Diary, I don't know which was more pleasing: the Priest family's wonderful offer . . . or *not* losing Arthur to some other place!

Later

I finally tracked down Retta and told her to get hold of Sidney and come to my apartment as soon as possible. When they arrived, I poured out my news, and the three of us got busy.

Sidney didn't waste any time. He found Evalina Davis at her rooming house and discussed the Priests' proposal with her. There were some tears, Sidney told me, but also relief. She has met the Priests and knows what good people they are.

Retta and I went to the hospital, saw the children, and found out that they can be released in the morning now that there will be folks to tend to the burns. While I read Jeff and Jamie some stories, Retta disappeared. On our way back to FairAcres, she told me that she had made an initial payment on the Davis account and had arranged with the business office to cover the remaining balance. We hope the generosity of residents on Storytelling Night will accomplish that.

I stopped by to see Arthur and tell him what had happened so far.

171

"Mr. Metcalf just called me," he reported. "He's gonna bring the boys' mother over this evenin' to talk to me and Dollie. Miz McNair, you and your friends are . . . well, I don't know how to describe it. You're . . . a band of angels."

I told Arthur that this angel was going upstairs and take off her wings and her shoes and have a cup of chamomile tea and a nap!

November 27th

So much has happened over this Thanksgiving holiday that I'll probably forget to put down some of it. The "bottom line" (as my children say) is that there are a lot of people around here with plenty to be thankful for.

The little burn victims are happily ensconced at Kudzu Kottage. If their appetites are any indication, they are well on the road to mending, according to Arthur.

Yesterday afternoon, Mrs. Davis left on a bus to Spartanburg. If all goes as hoped, she will live with her cousin and get employment at the mill. Sidney and Retta think that she sincerely wants to get her life together, and she has promised the Priests that she will send them money regularly.

After Christmas, I'm going to write an old business associate of Sam's who lives in Spartanburg and ask him and his wife if they will get in touch with Evalina and be of some help if needed. It seems much more desirable to handle this situation privately and avoid involving any official

172

agencies unless they are needed.

The Storytelling Night is still planned for Friday. Chris and Paul have taken on all the organizing, with extra support from the staff who have gotten caught up in the spirit of things. Mr. and Mrs. Detwiler are inviting some special friends to come to the dinner (supper, really) at The Home that night and stay for the event.

November 28th

This afternoon, Retta and I were having a glass of wine in my apartment.

"Do you know something, Hattie?" she said. "The way Sidney has handled this whole Davis family situation has been *masterful!*"

I nodded sagely. "Has he proposed yet?"

Retta actually blushed.

"Only about nineteen times," she said, with a slightly embarrassed smile. "Oh, I wish he wouldn't push me so! I'll own that I enjoy his attention — going out to dinner and to movies and things — and sometimes just driving around. He's what I call a graceful driver. No jerks. Just smooth and easy."

She paused thoughtfully. "I'll have to admit it's nice being 'squired around,' having a protective arm nearby —"

"Sounds like a lot of plusses to me. Can you name any minuses?"

"We're *old.*" She frowned, and gave me a puzzled look. "It doesn't seem *right.*"

173

"Right-schmight," I countered. "I'll tell you something, my friend. There are 'old' people — and then there are people who have reached a mellow kind of maturity that I, for one, find attractive! They don't expect too much from life. They live one day at a time — gratefully — absorbing, in a gentle way, all the good things that are still available and giving back good things to those around them . . . Whew! How I do run on! But it seems to me that Sidney Metcalf is a prime example of the best kind of 'growing old gracefully.' "

Retta nodded.

"How would you grade him on companionship?" I asked.

She grinned a little sheepishly. "With an A+, of course. You *knew* I'd have to say that." She sipped her wine and added, "He would deserve that grade. He seems to know exactly when to be quiet, when to reminisce, when to laugh, when to take charge . . . when to just *be* there."

"We should be taping this conversation," I laughed. "We could make a recording and call it 'The Paragon.' "

"He's not perfect, Hattie. He doesn't like seafood — though he takes me out for it — and he doesn't play bridge, and he doesn't have the nicest children in the world."

"You wouldn't have to see much of them."

"I know."

"Anything else?"

"Well," Retta hesitated. "There's the business

of making comparisons. I might not live up to his memories of his first wife."

"Listen, honey. I knew her. She was a very fine lady. If she hadn't been nice, he wouldn't want another spouse. But illness took its toll. The last few years of her life, she was a wreck. You must seem like Miss America to him. Young and gorgeous."

"Oh, Hattie, *do.*"

"What about your memories of Hal? Would you be making comparisons?" I persisted.

"You know, it's the same kind of story. Many good memories — but those last five years, with Hal partially paralyzed — Oh, dear, I don't *think* I'd be hard to please, now. . . .

"But, Hattie! So much has happened, so fast. There I was, leading the quiet life I'd led for years. Then came the upheaval of getting out of my house — my home for years and years — and coming to this new place — so very new to me — meeting what seemed like *thousands* of new people . . . and, right away, I was being courted! I'm not — what's the word? Precipitate? Impetuous? I'm more like the dull old tortoise."

"Uh-huh. You look like one, too," I said, smiling.

I stayed quiet for a moment, and then decided to plunge on. "There's something else to think about: the matter of loneliness. Oh, I know, we have plenty of *company* here; but I'm talking about — what do they call it these days? — a 'significant other' — to share experiences with,

175

and private jokes, and laughs, and troubles . . . to keep off the gloom of old-age loneliness that comes even when there are people close by.

"They're nice people," I said, "but they're not *ours*. Not body-close companions — as close and familiar as our own skins. You know what I mean . . . Lord, Retta! You've got a chance in a million! Don't throw it away willy-nilly, dear. You might be sorry."

She didn't answer; just looked out of the window into the distance.

I'd always known that Retta was not a gregarious person. She did not make dozens of friends in college, just a few that she selected carefully and kept, through thick and thin. We met and became friends through the Wild Thyme Literary Society. I remember liking a poem she wrote. It had a striking title: "My Friendship's Aristocracy."

I watched her now. Even with a frown of frustration, her face was a picture. Oh, to age softly like that! It was easy to see why Sidney had been captivated.

She finished her wine, still looking troubled. "I've always hated making decisions," she said, "and this one is so *serious*."

But a few minutes later, when we found her suitor waiting for us at the dining room door, Retta's eyes lit up at the sight of him. No doubt about it. I saw it plainly. I now have high hopes.

I have spent today wracking my brain and plundering my library trying to come up with my contribution for Storytelling Night tomorrow. There is one silly and slightly risqué story that keeps coming to mind, but I'm not really sure I want it to be my contribution to the evening.

This didn't happen at our Home. I'm not sure that it really happened at all; but I'll put down the tale just as it was given to me. (Maybe it'll go in the sequel!)

Julius, a resident of a retirement center, came out on the porch after supper, dressed to the nines, and obviously impressed with himself.

"Well, aren't you the dressed-up one," said Flora, the only other person on the porch.

He smirked. "I look OK, don't I? I'll bet you can't guess how old I am."

"I'll bet I can," said Flora. "I can if you'll do three things."

"What are they?"

"First, drop your pants."

Julius unbuckled his belt and let his trousers fall.

"Now, turn the other way."

Julius turned around.

"Now, drop your drawers," ordered Flora.

Julius dropped his drawers.

"You're eighty-one," announced Flora.

"How did you know?!" Julius asked incredulously, scrambling to cover himself and regain his dignity.

"You told me yesterday."

I also heard an anecdote at lunch today that I should also note down for future use. (It's more touching than funny.)

A lady on G Hall has been worried about her clothes closet. It hadn't had a really thorough cleaning since she'd moved here seven years ago. She is not able, now, to do the job herself.

Yesterday, she said, she arranged for someone in housekeeping to empty the closet, vacuum thoroughly, and put everything she wanted to keep back in neatly.

As she finished telling us the story, she sighed with satisfaction. "Now I can die and not be embarrassed!"

We could all identify with her sentiments.

Later

I believe I've decided on my story for tomorrow night, Dear Diary. I'll sleep on the idea tonight and read it again in the morning with a fresh eye.

Once again, the busybody genes have been working overtime around here. We have certainly gotten ourselves involved, for better or worse, in the lives of several people. I have to believe it's for better. . . . For two little boys, at least, I *know* it is.

I wish I could be as sure what to do about Retta and Sidney — if anything.

Chapter 12

A Night to Remember

December 1st (Late!)

Storytelling Night was a big success. That's all I have the energy to report. In eight minutes the clock will reach midnight, and I intend to be tucked up gratefully in my warm bed. Details tomorrow!

December 2nd

Despite last night's excitement, I slept like a log. It's no wonder, with all the activity of the past few weeks. This Poor Old Soul and some others, too, have been very busy!

Now, details, as promised — from the beginning.

The dining room was decorated with fresh holiday greenery, red bows, and candles. We had a big crowd, including two tables of guests hosted by Mr. and Mrs. D.

After the supper dishes were cleared away, coffee and Christmas cookies were served. Then Christine Summers greeted everyone from the temporary stage and lectern (for which someone had made a beautiful, old-fashioned boxwood wreath with a big red satin bow). Chris reminded us of why we were there, and then said:

"I'll start things off by reading something that I'm sure all of you heard many times in your childhoods, the story of Brer Rabbit and the Tar-Baby, by Joel Chandler Harris. It pains me that the Uncle Remus stories are heard so seldom today. Besides being delightfully funny, they are full of homely philosophy. This is probably the one you remember best."

Christine has a great voice, for singing and for reading, and a great ear for dialect. I sat there with my eyes brimming. She took me back to a fireside, with me sitting in my mother's lap, and with my brother sitting on the floor at our feet.

The book Mama held, *Nights with Uncle Remus*, was dog-eared. Every time Mama read that Brer Rabbit "hauled off" and hit the Tar-Baby, my brother would jam his right fist into his left hand. He would pretend that he couldn't get it loose.

By the time Christine read, "I hear Miss Sally callin', honey. You'd better run along," I was dissolved in tears.

Look here, Hattie, this won't do. Your turn is coming. Straighten up, gal.

The audience gave Chris a standing ovation — something that doesn't happen here too often

181

(it being a little hard for us to stand up and clap at the same time, dropping things like flashlights and programs and cough drops and Kleenexes).

Bill Nixon came on next.

"That's a hard act to follow, Christine. I wish I had taken time to look up something really good. . . . Anyway, this is a story I heard a long time ago, when people studied and understood Latin more than they do today.

"At a stylish dinner party there was a dreadful accident. The waiter, bringing in a tray bearing the entrée, a beef tongue, slipped and fell, spilling the meat on the floor. But the host, a man of letters, quickly turned the confusion into a *coup*.

"He smiled and said, 'Think nothing of it, my friends. That was just a *lapsus linguae*.'

" 'How clever!' said several of the guests. They even applauded their host's erudite aplomb.

"One of the guests had not studied Latin, and did not know that the phrase meant, 'a slip of the tongue,' but seeing their impressive effect on the other guests, she stored up the words in her memory.

"Later on, she gave a dinner party. She arranged for the waiter to slip and fall, dropping the *pièce de résistance*. The guests gasped, but the hostess smiled and said nonchalantly, 'Think nothing of it, my friends. That was just a *lapsus linguae*.' But to her amazement, nobody clapped or laughed. You see, the entrée was not a beef tongue; it was a baked chicken!"

182

Bill sat down to applause and laughter (and a few blank looks from those who didn't hear, or didn't "get," the language joke), and Austin made his way to the microphone.

"This story was put down by a man way back in the 'dark ages' — about 1925," Austin explained. "Otherwise it would say 'vest' instead of 'waistcoat.' Anyway, I'll read it."

"A prosperous-looking gentleman, sporting a huge watch chain across his waistcoat, was asked by a young man, riding beside him in the train, what time it was.

" 'I won't tell you!' snapped the older man.

" 'For goodness sake, why not?'

"Came this answer, all in one breath: 'Because if I tell you what time it is, you'll ask me my name and my business, and then to be courteous I'll have to ask you yours, although I'm not a damned bit interested; then you'll want to know where I live; and then you'll offer me a drink, and I'll have to offer you one; and presently I'll be getting off at Sudbury, where I live, and you'll get off there, too, and I'll have to ask you to my home for dinner, and you'll accept; and then you'll try to flatter my wife in order to get in right with her; and then you'll try to get in good with my daughter, and then Heaven knows what will happen — and *I don't want any man to marry my daughter who doesn't own a watch!*' "

When the laughter died down, Austin said, "That was such a quickie, I'll tell you another short one. This one's about two old ladies. Know

183

any of those?" People smiled and looked at each other.

"One old lady named Sadie went to see her friend, another old lady named Sallie, and found her dejected and crying.

" 'What are you cryin' about?' asked Sadie.

" 'I'll tell you what I'm cryin' about,' said Sallie. 'All my friends — all the ones I grew up with — are dead.'

" 'So what,' said Sadie. 'All my old friends are dead, too.'

" 'But you see,' said Sallie, 'all *my* friends are in heaven, and they're gonna look around for me, and when they don't find me, *they'll think I'm in the other place.*' "

Austin came down from the stage chuckling. He had enjoyed the telling of his tales so much that we had to applaud the hearing of them.

Marcia Coleman took the stand next.

"This is a true story, from my home town. The lady involved was married, but everybody called her Miss Trudy. That was the way in those days, especially in small towns in the South. I've written it out, to keep my tongue and memory from getting tangled."

Marcia opened her notebook, cleared her throat, and began to read:

"A nice elderly lady in my town made a tremendous decision for her time of life — the seventies — and for the *anno Domini:* circa 1935. She bought a car. It was said that while Miss

184

Trudy did not regret her decision, the local company that sold her the car did. They rued the day because, you see, teaching her to drive that shiny Buick was, alas, a part of the deal.

"After great danger to life and limb, and excessive wear and tear on his nervous system, the salesman gave up on teaching her to 'back' the car. He said she would just have to go forward, and that right slowly.

"She asked him to tie a string around the top of the steering wheel, so she would know when it was in the proper position. She also had him print on a piece of cardboard, in a large hand, the following instructions:

1. Be sure the gear-shift is in 'Neutral.'
2. Turn ignition key.
3. Press starter.
4. Press left foot on clutch.
5. Put gear-shift stick into first gear (left rear).
6. Ease up on clutch (left foot).
7. Put right foot on accelerator *gently*.

"When Miss Trudy decided she wanted to do some shopping at Alexander's Store on the town square, she would phone the store and ask if there was a parking place in front. A clerk would go outside and look for two adjoining parking places, knowing it would take that many. If she went back to the phone and said, 'Yes, ma'am,' Miss Trudy would say, 'Hold it for me.' So the clerk would go outside again and stand there and 'shoo off' any would-be parkers, until Miss Trudy rolled in with a great thump of tires against the curb.

"When her shopping was finished, Miss Trudy would ask a clerk to 'back' the car into the street for her (all parking in our town then was 'on the slant'), and then she would say, 'Turn off the key.'

"When the clerk got out of the car, Miss Trudy would get in and make sure that the string was at the top of the steering wheel, and then she would start down the checklist on her card: 1 . . . 2 . . . 3 . . . 4 . . . 5 . . . 6 . . . 7, and roar off home."

Marcia looked up at her audience, held up her right hand, and said, "It happened. Girl Scout's honor. I saw her do it — more than once."

She came down from the stage to loud laughter and applause. It was a typical Southern story, and we loved it.

It came my turn. I stood up and realized that my skirt was hiked up in front. Oh, me. Most old ladies have little (or sometimes big) "pots," which cause our skirts to be shorter in the front. *Tacky.* I call us "the potted ladies." I gave my skirt a pull-down, and went up on the stage.

"I'm going to read you a condensation of one of the most popular American short stories: 'The Gift of the Magi,' by William Sidney Porter, better known as O. Henry."

As usual, the tale of the young, impoverished

couple — of her cutting and selling her hair to buy him a watch chain for Christmas, while he sold his only prized possession, his watch, to buy combs for her magnificent hair — brought tears to many an eye in the audience.

I was pleased with the amount of applause, and with my selection.

There were a few more presentations, and then the evening moved toward its close with two fine storytellers.

"I'm going to tell you-all a yarn that could be titled 'Warts and All,' " said Ethel Minor, introducing the penultimate tale. Some of us smiled, knowing what was coming.

"You can smile," she said, "but this is true. It's medical history. I'm a digital guinea pig." She held up her hands and turned them round showing the fronts and backs.

"I don't know whether or not a toad frog caused them, but all through my childhood I had ugly warts on both hands. To say I hated them is an understatement. I despised them. I learned to play 'Für Elise' on the piano, but I was ashamed to play it in front of anybody. Wherever I went I tried to keep my hands covered.

"Of course when I reached the horrible age of thirteen, I was almost a basket case. I just *knew* that no one in pants — only boys and men wore them in those days — would ever want to hold my warty hand.

"I nagged my mother until she finally took me

to our family doctor's office. He put on each ugly lump a solution straight from the fiery furnace of the Bad Place. I could see it burning holes in my hands. It smoked and smelled. I gritted my teeth and bore the pain. *Any*thing for popularity.

"But, alas! Within weeks the warts reared their hideous heads again. Back I went to the doctor. He repeated his torture, but to no avail. The warts returned; and when they defied a third burning, the doctor scratched his head and said, 'I give up!'

"The following summer I was visiting relatives in a small town in Georgia when I heard about Aunt Mollie and her magic powers. I went to her unpainted house, which sat behind chinaberry trees in a clean-swept yard on the edge of town. I was a little nervous, but not after she came to the door, smiling and pleasant — no peaked hat, no broom.

" 'Zackly how many warts you got, honey?' she asked.

" 'Eleven,' I said.

" 'Well, I'll tell you whut. You gimme one penny for each wart. You shore about the number? It's got t'be right.'

"I counted again, and then gave her two nickels and a penny.

" 'Now you stop worryin',' she said. 'I'm gonna be busy this week and nex' week, choppin' cotton; but I'll git to work on yo' pesky warts week after nex'.'

" 'But I'll be going home. Won't I have to come back?'

" 'No, missy. You jes watch yo' hands, week after nex', an' you'll see them ugly things goin' away.' She grinned at me and waved as I went out of her gate.

"And do you know what? As the Lord is my witness, week after next those warts started drying up! Pretty soon they were only faint scars on fingers now fit to wear a swapped high school ring, or a fraternity ring, or — oh, joy! — even a wedding ring!

"I've wondered and wondered about the mystery of Aunt Mollie's powers. No one was ever able to explain it to me. All I know is, my parents had paid that torturing sawbones many dollars for nothing. I paid her eleven cents, and not a wart ever came back." She held up her hands again, and we gave her a big ovation.

Paul Chapin, the co-organizer with Christine, was the last storyteller. As had some others, he clutched a special section of an old newspaper.

"This tale is supposed to be true," he said. "Any of you who are from North Carolina have probably heard it. It's called 'Minnie Lawson and Her Famous Mule.' It attempts to explain how a candidate for sheriff of Chowan County, thought to be a shoo-in, lost the race.

"It seems that Mrs. James Lawson, now deceased, called Dr. Satterfield in Edenton from her farm home in Chowan County one evening about her mule, Horace. She was upset, and said, 'Doctor, Horace is sick, and I wish you would come look at him.'

"Dr. Satterfield said, 'Oh, Minnie, it's after six o'clock and I'm eating supper. Give him a dose of mineral oil, and if he isn't all right in the morning I'll come and take a look at him.'

"She wanted to know how to give Horace the mineral oil, and the doctor said it should be administered through a funnel. Mrs. Lawson protested that the mule might bite her, and Dr. Satterfield, a mite exasperated, said, 'Oh, Minnie, you're a farm woman and you know about these things. Give it to him through the other end.'

"Minnie went down to the barn, and there stood Horace, moaning and groaning and hanging his head. She looked for a funnel, but the nearest thing she could find was her Uncle Bill's fox-hunting horn hanging on the wall. This was a beautiful gold-plated instrument, with gold tassels.

"She took the horn and nervously affixed it properly. Horace paid no attention.

"Then she reached up on the high shelf where the medicines for the farm animals were kept. Instead of picking up the mineral oil, however, she grabbed a bottle of turpentine by mistake, and she poured a liberal dose of it into the horn.

"Horace raised his head with a sudden jerk. He let out a bray that could have been heard a mile down the road. He reared up on his hind legs, brought his front legs down, knocked out one side of the barn, cleared a five-foot-high fence, and started down the road at a mad gallop. Horace was in pain; every few strides he made, the horn would blow.

"All the dogs in the neighborhood knew when that horn was blowing it meant Uncle Bill was going fox hunting. So out on the road they tore, following close behind Horace.

"People who witnessed the chase said later that it was an unforgettable sight. First, Horace running at top speed with a horn in a most unusual position, the mellow notes issuing therefrom, the gold tassels waving, and the dogs barking joyously.

"They passed by the home of Old Man Leroy Dickenson, who was sitting on his front porch. He hadn't drawn a sober breath in fifteen years, and he gazed in fascinated amazement at the sight which unfolded itself before his eyes. He couldn't believe what he was seeing. Incidentally, Old Man Dickenson is said to be head man now in Alcoholics Anonymous in the Albemarle section of the state.

"By the time it was good and dark, Horace and the dogs were approaching the Inland Waterway. The bridge tender heard the horn blowing and figured that a boat was on the way. He hurried out and cranked up the bridge.

"Horace went overboard and drowned. The pack of dogs also went into the water, but they all swam out without too much difficulty.

"Now it happened that the bridge tender was the favorite candidate running to unseat the sheriff of Chowan County, but he managed to poll

Horace was in pain; every few strides he made, the horn would blow.

only seven votes, and these were all from kinfolks. Those who took the trouble to analyze the election results said the people there figured that any man who didn't know the difference between a mule with a horn up his caboose and a boat coming down the Inland Waterway wasn't fit to hold any public office in the county!"

Those of us who hadn't heard that saga whooped over it. Those who had heard it before had another good laugh at the thought of the poor animal's predicament.

That was the last of the stories. Paul thanked all the storytellers and all the appreciative listeners. Then he called on Sidney to bring everyone up to date on the boys and Mr. Stringfellow.

Sidney got up from the back where he and Retta had been helping to host Mr. Detwiler's company, and made his way up to the microphone.

"As I think all of you know," he started, "we're here to help two small children who have been hurt through no fault of their own. Mr. Stringfellow was hurt too — making his heroic rescue — but I'm glad to report that he is coming along well in the Veterans' Hospital, and he expects to be home after Christmas. We will arrange for someone to stay with him until he gets his strength back. His remarkable spirit is already coming back."

Sidney continued, "But it's for Jeffrey and Jamie Davis that we are really here tonight — to help defray their hospital expenses. They've enjoyed all the presents you good people have sent them; but now, money is needed."

Then Sidney told the audience all about the Priests' wonderful offer.

"The boys are already settled in, and they are recuperating quickly. Their mother is in Spartanburg, already employed at a mill, and living with her cousin. Mrs. Gooding and I have come to feel much better about Mrs. Davis, and we think she will work hard to pick up the pieces of her life. Her poor mother's death actually lifts a big burden from her shoulders. She has felt responsible for her mother for a long time . . . but that's another story, and, though tragically, that story has now ended.

"Anyway," Sidney moved ahead, "Arthur and Dollie want to give the boys a home for as long as they need one. They plan to have Mr. Stringfellow over, on weekends, as soon as he is able to come. That will please the Davis boys.

"So, dear people: Think about those two little appealing faces, and open up your hearts and pocketbooks. We want to pay their doctor's bills and get them some new clothes. Everything they had was destroyed in the fire."

For an "offertory," two of our men had consented to perform duets of a crude sort on the piano. Neither one could read a note of music. Curtis plunked out chords in the bass with stubby fingers — THUMP-two-three, THUMP-two-three — while Bill Nixon picked out the melody in the treble and sang:

> "Oh where, oh where has my little dog gone?
> Oh where, oh where can he be?
> With his tail cut short and his ears cut long,
> Oh where, oh where can he be?"

They went on, verse after silly verse, while the money and checks piled up in the baskets. The wonderful people here are *so* generous.

When the collection was finished, Sidney thanked everyone again and called for a big hand for Christine and Paul who organized the evening. Then, as the clapping died away and the rustling of departures began, Sidney held up his hand and said, "I would like to take this opportunity to make what, to me, is a very delightful announcement."

We perked up our ears. Several people went: "Sh-h-, sh-h-h, *listen* —" and the room quieted back down.

Sidney beamed. "Mrs. Henrietta Gooding has decided, as of today, to accept my proposal of marriage!" He smiled at Retta, who sat in the back blushing. "The wedding will take place two weeks from today, at three o'clock, in the chapel, and we hope all of you will attend."

There was clapping and foot-stomping, and even whistling. Real rejoicing. It seemed to me they were saying, "*See,* Cupid, we're not dead yet!"

Sidney came down from the stage. Mr. Detwiler escorted Retta to the front to join him, so that people could congratulate them together. It was a happy way to end the evening. I was so pleased. Maybe I didn't godmother the match, but I had certainly encouraged it. I'm convinced that these two people are compatible, and will enrich each other's lives — and maybe some of the shine will rub off on the rest of us!

So now, with the fire victims taken care of and the romance nicely resolved, I can get back to the serious business of writing questions for the C.Q. test. Maybe I will find time to do something about the nation's debt, too. My congressman answered my letter, and he is coming to see me next Thursday!

Life, for a while, will go on. *Deo volente.*

About the Author

Effie Leland Wilder's first novel, OUT TO PAS-TURE, was published to great acclaim in 1995 when she was eighty-five years old. She has lived in Summerville, South Carolina for fifty-six years, the last nine of them at The Presbyterian Home of Summerville. She graduated from Converse College in 1930, and received the Distinguished Alumna Award in 1982. She has also received the Order of the Palmetto, South Carolina's highest award, for her philanthropic work.

Her writing has been published in the *Charleston News and Courier* and the *Saturday Evening Post*, and she is the co-author of PAWLEY'S ISLAND: A LIVING LEGACY. She is the widow of Frank Page Wilder, and has three sons, a daughter, and seven grandchildren.

About the Illustrator

Laurie Allen Klein's illustrations have appeared in OUT TO PASTURE (BUT NOT OVER THE HILL) as well as in *Atlanta Magazine* and *Athens Magazine*. Klein, her husband, and her daughter live in Madison, Georgia.

The employees of G.K. Hall hope you have enjoyed this Large Print book. All our Large Print titles are designed for easy reading, and all our books are made to last. Other G.K. Hall books are available at your library, through selected bookstores, or directly from us.

For information about titles, please call:

(800) 257-5157

To share your comments, please write:

Publisher
G.K. Hall & Co.
P.O. Box 159
Thorndike, ME 04986